To Have and To Hold

Switched at Marriage, Episode 3

Gina Robinson

Gina Robinson
SEATTLE, WASHINGTON

Book Layout ©2013 BookDesignTemplates.com

To Have and To Hold, Switched at Marriage 3/ Gina Robinson. — 1st ed.
ISBN 978-0692454435

For Jeff

ECHO BAY CHRISTMAS

CHAPTER ONE

Kayla

Mothers-in-law have a bad rep. On a scale of one to ten they rank a scant notch below the wicked stepmother for general mayhem-causing and malevolent intentions. In family dynamics, they're always that wrench that screws everything up. The stereotype has always been the guy with the poisonous mother-in-law. But my married girlfriends swore the opposite was true—the guy's mom was ten to one the more controlling, conniving madwoman of the two mothers. The guy's mom had to fight against the truth of that old saying, "A daughter's a daughter all her life. A son's a son until he takes a wife."

As I stood in the foyer of Justin's luxury penthouse, ambushed by the mother-in-law my new husband had assured me I wouldn't even have to meet, I sided with my girlfriends on this one. Diana Green, and her icy "we have to talk," fit the stereotype completely. She was staring at me, waiting for me to either answer or flinch. The metaphoric ball was in my court.

I glanced around, looking for Magda and *help*! Naturally, she was nowhere in sight. Not like she was on my side, anyway. But I held out the faint hope her presence would restrain Justin's mom from using the full force of her artillery. Data barked happily and came running to me, one joyful spot of puppy in the building gloom. I scooped her up and cuddled her to me.

"If you're looking for Justin's housekeeper, I gave her the afternoon off." Diana Green didn't rise from the sofa to greet me. "I need to talk with you, *privately*."

Privately was never a good thing. We were off to an infamously bad start. On top of everything else, I was going to have to put a stop to Diana's sense of entitlement. She couldn't just barge in here unannounced and potentially blow our cover. No, I couldn't risk that. I would have to make it clear—I ran Justin's house now. For his protection.

I'd never met Justin's parents or brothers. He hadn't talked about them more than in passing when we were in college. Why would he? It's not like college kids sit around talking about their parents. Parents are the last thing anyone wants to think about. So I had no idea what to expect. I hadn't seen so much as a picture of them. I was at as much of a disadvantage as Diana was.

Each of us were surprised strangers. There was only one thing to do—kill her with kindness.

I plastered a smile on my face and walked over to tower over where she sat on the sofa. Well, not exactly tower. Even sitting, she was a surprisingly tall woman. "I'm Kayla." I smiled as warmly as I could and extended my hand.

She ignored it.

"I know who you are." Her eyes were still hard and suspicious. Measuring, as she studied me.

It wasn't as if I blamed her for being suspicious. Our sudden marriage had to be a shock, a sort of surprise attack. But I was tired of being branded the villainess for helping Jus out of a jam. And banned from explaining. How did spies not blow their covers every single day? Life was *so* not fair.

In a weird way, I was actually happy she'd showed up. It at least proved she was concerned about her son. Her initial casual lack of worry had struck me as indifferent. Had I been her, I would have been on the first plane back, too. But I wondered how Justin had misread her so easily.

I stared at her, trying to see any similarities between her and her son, physical or otherwise. Diana sat tall and regally, back straight. If I had to guess, I would say she was late fifties. Slender. Fit. Short, dark hair without any gray, the kind of cut older women favored. Obviously colored, but nicely done. Her makeup was light, natural looking. She wore slacks and a blouse that bordered on athletic wear, and serviceable flats, not heels. Her shoulders were surprisingly square, as was her jaw.

She had an almost mannish look, but was at the same time striking. Not beautiful. But arresting. Interesting to look at. She was the kind of woman who reminded you, at least in attitude, of your high school PE teacher. Or the girls' volleyball coach. Or maybe the school's athletic director. Picture her with a whistle around her neck and you pretty much got the idea.

It was hard to imagine the scrawny Justin I'd known in college as her son. Even the grownup Jus was more slightly built than his mom, and about the same height. She had to be nearly six feet tall. They both had dark hair and eyes. And yes, I could see a similarity around the eyes. Maybe Justin had her square jaw beneath that beard. But who knew for sure.

Was Diana a coach or something? It struck me that I had no idea what she and Justin's dad did for a living. Or where she'd hopped on her broom and flown back from.

"You must have had a long trip. Can I get you something?" I was trying my best to be hospitable, even though there was already a drink on the coffee table in front of her.

She arched an eyebrow. "I have one already." She made it sound like I was stupid for not noticing. The *This is my son's house and I can help myself to anything I want* was left unsaid, but clearly implied.

"Obviously," I said with a smile. "But I'd be happy to refresh it."

"That's kind of you. But no, thank you." Her voice softened ever so slightly as she watched me pet Data. It was as if the dog liking me was at least one small point in my favor.

I took a seat in the chair opposite her and settled Data in my lap. *Let the wooing begin.* "I'm so glad you came! This is an unexpected surprise. Does Justin know you're here? He didn't seem to think you'd be home soon."

She laughed at that, actually laughed. It was the feminine version of Justin's, and surprisingly reassuring. "My baby boy is clearly clueless. The kid is smart as a whip, but socially awkward and naïve. He didn't really think I wouldn't be curious about his new bride and want to meet her immediately?"

I shook my head, sympathizing with her. Naively clueless was an apt description. "He said something about you being very busy this time of year and unable to break away from business?"

She rolled her eyes. "This *is* one of our busiest seasons, right up there with Thanksgiving and winter breaks. With the high schools and colleges getting out for the school year, our summer athletic tournament season swings into full gear." She sounded exasperated. "You have no idea what we do, do you?"

I smiled sweetly and shook my head. "No, sorry."

"We own Rugby Explorers. We arrange international tournaments and travel for high school and college rugby teams, both men's and women's. Our tournaments are run on school breaks in exotic locales. Summer is exceptionally hectic for us. I had to come back from Italy just now, leaving Justin's dad and our staff shorthanded. We employ about fifty people. Justin's two older brothers work for us. Are partners, in fact. It's a family business. Everyone but Justin is involved." She didn't sound happy about that, not at all. As if Justin was the black sheep for being wildly successful on his own.

"Justin is the odd duck of our brood. Has been since the day he was born, little and scrawny with a thatch of unruly dark hair. The other two boys were bald as billiard balls at birth. Looking at them now, you wouldn't know it." She took a quick breath. Her face softened at the thought of her older boys. They were clearly the apples of her eyes.

"I would love to see a baby picture of Jus!" I really would. I was hoping we could bond over adorable baby memories.

Her face hardened. She ignored my request. Jus wasn't her favorite. "Justin *would* sneak off and get married when he thought I was distracted and not paying attention to what he's up to. He's always had a knack for timing things to get away with them."

She sighed, heavily, as if her youngest son was the bane of her existence and a total puzzle to her. As if any son who didn't want to travel the globe arranging rugby tourneys was no son of hers. "He wouldn't want my opinion, in any case. Certainly not the opinion he knew I would give him."

The tone she used was the same one coaches used when they lectured you for missing the shot that would have won the game.

"I would have stopped him from making this idiotic rash decision." She tilted her head, waiting for my reaction with glittering eyes. She looked as if she was aching for a fight.

She wasn't one to mince words. I actually sort of appreciated her candor. At least I knew where I stood. I felt just as defensive and protective of Jus.

"I would have, too!"

Her eyebrows shot up into her hairline.

Crap. I forgot my role too easily. The thought of that squinky identity thief taking advantage of Jus made me irrationally angry. I would have stopped him, too. If I'd been there when she'd conned him. Or drugged him. Or whatever she'd done to bend him to her will. "If I'd been his mom. Marry in haste. Repent at leisure—"

Even when someone else had married in your name, as I was learning all too well. I was still thinking about Lazer. And ruing that I hadn't met *him* earlier. Given a choice, I would have *never* run off and gotten married on a drunken whim. I was married to a billionaire and I hadn't gotten so much as a fabulous wedding out of the deal.

She frowned, looking as if she thought I was mocking her. Lucky for me she took my mistake the wrong way and couldn't see the truth of the situation. But then, who expected an imposter bride? Jus and I had that element of the unexpected in our favor. Which came in handy when I nearly screwed up.

"But our marriage isn't as hasty as it seems," I continued, lying my pants off. "Justin and I *have* known each other since early college days."

"Yes," she said, dryly. "I know *he* had a crush on *you* in college. You were all he could talk about in his blushing, boyish way. Justin has always been awkward around girls." Her gaze was piercing, accusing, as if I had led him down the path to ruin with my vast experience and siren ways.

The thought of Jus pining for me was...oddly touching. At the same time, I felt like a voyeur prying into his private life. Because we were married, his mom obviously felt comfortable sharing his obsession with me now. Because it had so obviously paid off. Maybe she even thought I would be flattered and touched. As in, *Awwww, he's loved me forever!* Girly squeal. Pattering heart.

She didn't know she was giving me info I wasn't entitled to, and that would embarrass Jus.

She gave me a pointed look and sighed. "Unrequited, as I recall." Her gaze held mine, as if she was looking for faults and weaknesses. Anything she could exploit. "Money makes a man *so* much more attractive, don't you think, Kayla?"

Oh, damn. So there it was.

"I didn't marry Jus for his money!" I really hadn't. Not exactly. But my protest, though heartfelt, tumbled with a feeble plunk into the airspace between us. I'd married Jus for the independence it would give me after this year of fakery was over. And to help him out, of course.

With any luck, if I could convince Diana of my sincerity maybe she would disappear back to that Italian rugby tournament. Disappear for the rest of our agreed-upon year of marital whatever this was. Leave us alone. And I wouldn't have to see her again.

I probably should have professed my undying love for her son right then and there. Hammed it up and laid it on thick. Argued with her. Protested. I was supposed to be an over-the-moon newlywed. But Diana was a no-nonsense person. I decided it was better to appeal to her rational side. And tell as much of the truth as possible.

"You're entitled to your opinion. And concerns. I'll obviously have to prove myself to you over time. But you should know that I didn't jump at Justin's money. He had to convince *me* to marry *him*. Whatever you believe about me—I am *good* for Jus."

That second part was the absolute truth. In so many ways I would never be able to explain.

She studied me, but didn't give away whether she believed me or not. "No gushy protests about how much you love my boy?" She laughed, softly, cynically.

"What's the point? You're not in a mind frame to believe me."

"You're right." There was just the slightest glint of admiration in her eyes. "You're smart. And savvy. You read people well. And you're rational. I'm pleased to see all that, at least. I didn't necessarily expect Justin to marry an airhead. But you *never* know with him. He has a habit of doing the exact opposite of what we expect. Or want."

The "like marrying you" was implied.

She took a sip of her drink, looking as if she *really* needed it. And maybe something even stiffer. I knew how she felt. I needed a drink, too. But I needed a clear head more.

"Let's be honest with each other. My youngest son has never been God's gift to women. Not like his older brothers. The girls have always fallen over them. Since preschool. Those two boys have charm and charisma enough for an army. Justin, however..."

She rolled her eyes and studied me again. "He isn't the kind of boy a girl *like you* would usually go for, is he?"

I didn't like the implications of that "like you." As if I was some lower form of scammer.

I kept my head high and my voice as sweet as I could, hating myself for playing dumb. "I don't know what you mean. Jus is completely adorable. Sweet and thoughtful—"

"And not at all the bad-boy jock, like your last boy-friend?" She laughed. "Yes, I know about him. I've seen enough of the girls who hang around the athletes at our tournaments. You're *exactly* like one of their fangirls. If one of the older two boys had brought you home, I wouldn't have batted an eye. You're exactly their type and them yours. But Justin?" She couldn't stop shaking her head. "No. We expected that if he ever married it would either be to a nerd girl, like his friend Ophie, or to some beauty who only saw his dollar signs." She sighed again. "Ophie must be livid and heartbroken. They're two of a kind and spend an inor-dinate amount of time together. She's had her eye on my boy all along." Diana's laugh was anything but amused.

Would she have preferred Ophie for a daughter-in-law? I couldn't tell.

"I worried that one of the Flashionista girls would be conniving enough to catch him. That's what he was hoping for when he set up a company filled with girls." She laughed again, this time genuinely.

I didn't understand why that was so funny.

"Sorry. You're not in on the joke? Justin hasn't shared his geek's rules for getting the girl?" She shook her head, as if she was pleased with herself. "Rule number one—set up a target-rich environment. When Riggins came to Justin to talk him into joining him to start Flashionista, one of the main selling points was the heavily young, stylish, mostly female workforce they envisioned."

"Jus has rules for getting girls?" I didn't know why I found that so amusing. I pictured a young Jus watching a movie like *Hitch* for dating advice.

His mom thought she was insulting me. But she was giving me so much ammo against him. Not that I planned to use it. Why would I?

"When you're a scrawny, broke genius nerd, you can't rely on your good looks and charm. You have to stack the deck in your favor. Up your odds of success." Diana broke into a full-scale smile and covered her mouth, looking innocently as if she'd unwittingly let too much escape. "I shouldn't tell tales on my son and give away his secrets. His plan seemed to be working. The girls at Flashionista love him. There are plenty of them who will hate you for catching him."

Yes, I was sure there were plenty of girls who wanted a billionaire.

"Justin was always sensitive, always caring, and always trying to be like his big brothers." Diana turned suddenly serious. "But he came out of the womb different from his brothers from the beginning. They were both late, big babies, each over nine pounds. Jus was a tiny, sickly preemie. He started out life too early. If he hadn't been a genius, maybe he could have caught up eventually." She sighed with regret. "But no. The little bugger had to be so damned smart. He taught himself to read at two and a half."

I stared at her. "Two and a half?"

She nodded and shook her head. "No one ever believes me. People are always astonished. He read like a fourth grader right off the bat. At first I thought he was mimicking his brothers, memorizing what they were reading to him. But no, he read the newspaper to me one day and I knew we had to do something with him. So it was off to school early with him. And then the challenge of how many grades to skip him and how often. The curse of intelligence." She paused. "On top of it all, he had to be my late bloomer. He never has reached the height of his older brothers. He's still the runt."

I rushed to his defense. "He's six feet tall. He's filled out nicely!"

She smiled, as if she was finally pleased about something. "Good. Maybe my initial impression of this marriage will turn out to be wrong. I'm glad to see you defending him. You have to understand this about my baby boy—if I'm protective of him, it's because I have a right to be.

"When he was growing up, Justin was bullied, beaten, and teased mercilessly. Never picked for sports teams or at recess. Recess! Most kids' favorite class was torture for him. I was never gladder for middle school, because there was no damned recess."

She shuddered. "Just worse things, as I soon found out. Wedgied. Head stuck in toilets. Shoved in lockers. When he was a freshman in high school, at about twelve, some of the older boys stuffed him in a trash can. He'd probably mouthed off to them. Or shown them up in class. The problem with being as smart as Justin is that he unwittingly makes other people look and feel dumb. He can't help it. You can imagine how the older boys felt being shown up in class by a kid who should have still been in elementary school.

"Justin got a concussion. I had to take him to emergency. He got six stitches in his head. Still has a scar right at his hairline."

So that's how he got the scar, I thought.

"The boys were never caught. Jus refused to rat on them. Though if I know my boy, he got them back somehow. Justin has always lived by his wits. After that, he was more careful." She paused.

My heart broke for the young Jus. Kids could be so cruel. Even college kids. People used to make fun of him at the university, too. Even I wasn't *lily* white.

"If not for his wits and the protection of his older brothers, I don't think he would have survived childhood."

"Yes, but look at him now!" I smiled brightly. "He's a celebrity.

"Yes. Look at him *now*." Her gaze ran over me in way that said, *Married to a money-grubbing bimbo.*

CHAPTER TWO

Justin

Minutes before three o'clock, Ophie came into my office. "Justin, can you come to the cafeteria? Barry's asked for you to meet him there. There's some kind of facility emergency?"

Barry was our head of facilities. I'd been wondering what pretense the staff would use to get me to my surprise party. My calendar was suspiciously open, as if Ophie had cleared it on purpose. I got out of my desk chair. "All right. Hope it's nothing major."

"Me too. Hungry employees are angry employees." Ophie tagged along with me. "You don't mind if I come along? I could use an afternoon snack."

The cafeteria was on the second floor. My office was on the top floor, the fourth-floor corner office with a

view of Puget Sound and the Olympic Mountains. Of
the piers and the cruise and cargo ships coming in.

We headed for the stairs. I rarely took the elevator. I
preferred the exercise. As we walked past the ping-
pong and foosball tables in the middle of the floor, they
were also suspiciously empty.

Riggins and I insisted on creating a casual, fun
workplace for our employees. Patterning it, in our limited budget way, on the simpler perks of Silicon Valley
startups like Apple and Google back in the day. Crea-
tivity needs time to develop. Exercise fuels the brain. A
relaxed brain is a brain ready to create. That was our
theory. We encouraged our employees to take breaks.
Heated ping-pong games broke out regularly. We had
tournaments and allowed for modest betting in pools. I
resisted the urge to comment on the silence.

As we passed the third floor, the photography studi-
os were empty, too. We photographed our catalog,
which changed online daily, onsite. Ophie chatted
away, obviously trying to distract me so I wouldn't notice the lack of busy employees.

I was working on my surprised face as we came
down the stairs into the second floor cafeteria.

"Surprise!"

An eruption of confetti and streamers covered me.
My surprise at being covered in bits of paper was genuine. I was faking enough in my life. It was good to be
real about *something*.

The cafeteria was decorated like a wedding reception with props from the photography department—
candles, artificial flower arrangements, tablecloths, and

balloons. A congratulations banner hung across the far side of the room, running the length of a table in front of it with a several large sheet cakes and three layer cakes on tiers of various heights. Enough cake to feed a small army of Flashionista employees.

"What? Is all this for me?" I couldn't help grinning as I dusted confetti off my shoulders and the crowd of my employees applauded. I was a happy, horrendously sexually frustrated groom.

As I stepped from the last step into the cafeteria, I was mobbed with hugs and pats on the back. I made my way across the room. Girl after girl whispered congrats in my ear and kissed my cheek. I'd never been more popular.

Wylie, our chief of operations, waited for me at the table and handed me a knife. "Cut the cake, man."

"What's this for?" I asked as I took it, playing innocent. Then I saw the writing on the cake. *Congratulations on your marriage* was written in Flashionista blue on the highest sitting white layer cake. In the center was a ceramic wedding cake topper—a groom in a tux dancing with his bride and dramatically dipping her backward, as if he'd swept her off her feet. A much better quality topper, I might add, than the one Lazer had gotten.

I stroked my beard and pointed to the smooth face of the groom. "Who's this guy dancing with my bride? I'm not that suave."

Those around me laughed.

"It's a hint." Wylie slapped me on the back. "The girls think you should shave off that monstrous bush on your face. They're taking bets as to whether there's a weak chin under there or not. Guess the wife must like it."

Hardly.

"Suave? Are you kidding?" Harry stepped out of the crowd. "You swept a girl off her feet in a matter of days, if not hours."

Damn that Harry for teasing me. I ignored his jab.

Marla came up next to me. "Chill, bossman. The bakery didn't have any bearded cake toppers on such short notice. And yes, we all think you *are* that suave, Justin. Look at you! Marriage agrees with you." She tugged my shirt and made a circle around my head in the air with her finger. "New haircut. New clothes. Trimmed beard. Fixing up for her! Sweet. She's got you wrapped around her little finger. You're just the cutest billionaire around."

I *was* crazy for Kayla. I would dress any way Kayla wanted if it made her happy. It was easy to let it show. There was nothing fake about the way I felt about our marriage. Except for the way it had gone down and the celibate nature of it. "You're going to make me blush."

"That would be cute, too." Marla winked. "Why oh why didn't you fix up sooner, Justin? I would have loved to see you knock Lazer Grayson off Seattle's Hottest Bachelor list."

Yeah, he had a big head about that. The way Marla fluttered around me, I almost thought she was flirting.

Wylie raised a glass. "Lazer's place is safe now. To one less bachelor in our midst!"

Everyone in the crowd of Flashionista staff was holding a red plastic cup. Suddenly it felt a lot like college as they raised them to toast my marriage.

"To the happy couple." Marla lifted hers, too. "We have a surprise for you. Ladies?"

She directed our attention toward the wall of the cafeteria and the calendar of important events in Flashionista's history. Like its founding. When we hit one hundred employees. The date of our IPO. It was covered with pictures of employees and press shots. The art department maintained it. It was an impressive, highly creative project.

Two of our original merch buyers stood before it, holding a sheet in front of it, blocking it from view. On Marla's signal, they dropped the sheet and unveiled the latest entry.

The Jet City Billionaires' Club recognizes Flashionista cofounder Justin Green for his contributions to Flashionista's success and phenomenal growth. And the date signified with a pair of overlapping wedding rings. The words *Wedded to Success* were written below it.

I shook my head, embarrassed and pleased, as the crowd applauded again. "You guys are sneaky," I whispered to Marla. She knew I wouldn't allow my wedding on the calendar. "Thank you, everyone! This is...too much."

There was a present on the table. One of the photographers yelled at me to open it. "A little something to make the groom happy."

"Oh, shit," I whispered as I picked it up. It was too light to be anything appropriate. I opened it gingerly

and cautiously pulled out one of the skimpiest lingerie
sets—a thong panty and crop-top-cami-bra-type
thing—we'd ever featured on the site. I held the thong
out, dangling from one finger. "This looks suspiciously
like one of our samples."

Wylie shoulder-bumped me. "Yeah, well, it *was*
short notice. That's what happens when you elope and
there's no gift registry. What do you get the man who
has everything, anyway? This should give you a little
fun." He winked. "Debbie from housewares insisted the
coffee machine we've all been eyeing goes into the sample sale. So that was out."

Debbie overheard and put her hands on her hips,
giving him the death-ray glare. "Wylie, you big liar!
You never told me you wanted it *for Justin*. It's going
to bring top dollar for the children."

"Hey! We offered to pay." Wylie turned to me. "Justin, we took up a collection." He pointed to the panties
I was holding. "We paid sample sale prices for that fair
and square."

We sold ladies' clothes for four to ten dollars apiece
at the sample sale. So, yeah, maybe people dug deep
and threw in their pocket change for the max ten bucks
it cost. Still, I loved this group and their crazy sense of
loyalty and humor.

I clutched my heart. "I'm touched. You got me right
here. Am I supposed to snap this into the crowd for one
of you guys to catch?" I pulled it back and took aim.

The girls laughed. The guys jumped back, a parting
of the seas as if that tiny, sexy thong was the Ebola vi-
rus.

Marla grabbed it away from me before I snapped it like a rubber band. "Boys! This is a classy celebration. Cut the cake, will you? The natives are hungry."

I sliced a wedge out of the layer with the cake topper and flipped it onto a white paper dessert plate that looked suspiciously like the ones the cafeteria used. They'd obviously spared no expense. But they were creative. I looked around. "Someone's missing. Shouldn't there be a girl here, like my wife, to stuff cake in my mouth?"

One of the girls from marketing raised her hand. "I'll do the duties."

I backed up with my hand up in self-defense. "Yeah, I bet you will. Nothing like getting a legit chance to put a cake in the boss' face. No thanks!" I broke off a piece with my fingers and stuffed it in, getting frosting on my fingers and the corners of my mouth. "Satisfied? Let them eat cake!"

"When *do* we get to meet the bride?" a guy from transportation yelled to me.

"You would want to meet her," I shot back.

"Yeah, well, we're guessing she's prettier than you!"

I was pleased I had created an environment where the staff felt comfortable flipping me shit. "She is."

"So?" one of the merch buyers said. "Answer the question."

"At the next Flashionista happy hour party. I promise. Now someone just has to arrange one." I winked at one of the merch buyers. They were the usual party-planning suspects.

Marla picked up the cake knife. "Mingle with your kingdom and leave the cake cutting to the experts."

A line of well-wishers formed. I spent the next half-hour talking with employees as they grabbed cake and congratulated me. As people got their cake, they wandered back to their desks and work. I finally broke free and went back to my office.

I was feeling great about the company and the future. Confident. Happy I had such awesome employees and had created a fun work environment. I wouldn't admit it, but I was touched my employees had thrown me a jokey impromptu wedding party. Even though I knew they used any excuse to get cake.

As I closed my office door, my phone buzzed. I had a text from Kayla. A smile bloomed on my face. And withered when I read it. *Your mom's here.*

Shit! I could almost hear the desperation and plea in Kayla's voice to get home *now*.

I texted her back. *Be right there.*

My phone buzzed back immediately. Expecting it to be Kayla, I smiled. As I read it, my face fell and my mood went black.

The girl on the news is not the Kayla Green you married.

Kayla

Just as I thought I would slit my wrists if I were left alone with Justin's mom another minute, the penthouse door flew open and Jus strolled in as casually as the breeze. He was carrying a bag from a cellular store, a pink cake box, and a Flashionista mailer envelope.

Yes! The cavalry has arrived.

His face lit up when he saw me. The ham looked *exactly* like a new groom in love. He was *so* playing his mom. "Honey! I'm home!"

I jumped to my feet and ran to him, throwing myself into his arms completely for show. "And none too soon," I whispered before I pressed a kiss of genuine gratitude on his lips.

He wrapped his arms around me, cake box, cell phone bag, and mailer still in hand. And kissed me as if he was proving to his mom the validity of our marriage. It was all cake and roses. "I brought you a few little somethings. This first."

He handed me the bag from the cellular store. When I opened it, there was a new cell phone, all the accessories, and a new case. An expensive designer case.

His expression was as brilliant, hopeful, and warm as sunshine. "You other phone is dated. This one has all the latest features." He rattled them off in technical detail, still beaming.

I thanked him with another swift kiss.

"I'll transfer all your contacts and set it up for you later." He was still grinning. And making his mom wait for his attention, as if showing her I was the new top dog female in his life. "And this is a gift from my employees. For you to wear for me."

He handed me the mailer and set the cake box on the counter. "Mom! This is a surprise!"

I stepped back, out of the way, as he opened his arms to her. Diana rose from the sofa and hugged her boy. Justin was a scant inch taller than her. He hugged her enthusiastically, with boyish happiness. Seeing them together, they were more similar than I'd first thought. And seemed to have a real affection for each other, even if he wasn't her favorite.

While they hugged, I peeked into the mailer and gasped. It was the thong and cami set I'd been coveting when I'd seen it on Flashionista. I'd thought about buying it to surprise Eric. But even at the Flash's heavily discounted prices, it was out of my budget. I pulled out the lustrous silk satin and French leavers lace thong and ran my fingers over the fineness and quality of it. It was so soft and wonderful I wanted to put it on immediately. How had they guessed my size?

I pulled it gently from the bag where it had been haphazardly wadded and stuffed and hung it over one finger. Who abused fine lingerie like this? Jus was still embracing his mom, but he was watching me, gauging my reaction. Judging from his expression, he thought it was a joke. No way, big boy. This was fine stuff.

I crooked my finger at him and winked seductively. "I'll put this on for you later." I flashed him a smile full of promise. Oh, yeah. I was going to wear this. I couldn't wait to try it on.

His eyes lit with desire. And if I could have seen his Adam's apple, I'm sure it bobbed. I carefully folded the panties and put them back in the mailer next to the cami just as his mom released him and turned around.

"What did they get you?" she asked.

"Nothing, Mom." Poor baby, he looked embarrassed.

"Something for the honeymoon." I smiled sweetly at Diana, that smile girls give when they have the upper hand.

If this had been a real marriage, it would let her know her boy was *mine* now. I was the one sleeping with him. What mom could compete with sex? She couldn't know our marriage was a special, platonic case.

I was only pretending, but it felt delicious. I put the mailer under my arm and went to the counter to open the cake box. "More cake? Are they trying to fatten us up?"

I recognized the bakery name on the box—another of the finest bakeries in town. Known for their cakes. Jus was the billionaire here, but I wasn't certain he knew just what his employees had given him. I opened the box, and the cake was an absolutely gorgeous white cake with buttercream frosting covered with pink fondant and filled with raspberry rum filling. A slice was missing. The filling was oozing out.

I inhaled deeply. It was like ambrosia. It was also exactly the cake I would have picked. If I'd been getting married. In fact, it was pinned on my secret wedding Pinterest board. I let out a sigh that sounded almost sexual. That cake smelled like heaven and white chocolate. And sitting on top was the most romantic topper—a bride and groom dancing, with the groom dipping her. "I think I'm in love with your staff!"

"Another cake topper to add to our collection." Jus had released his mom and stood with his arm around her.

"Not *just* another cake topper. This is a premium cake topper from one of the premier ceramics manufacturers in the world! It's...well...it's pricey. I love it! We'll put it someplace special."

"You have a collection?" Diana looked confused.

"Lazer gave us one last night." Jus rolled his eyes.

"Enough said." Diana studied her son. "You're just in time. Dinner just arrived. I chased Magda off before she could cook. Kayla ordered out."

Her voice was neutral. I couldn't tell whether she was slamming my lack of cooking skills or not. I was a decent cook. But I needed some warning, time to shop and plan, and at least a rudimentary knowledge of where things were in the kitchen. Somehow Diana and I had muddled through and found what we needed to set the table.

Jus frowned. "What did you do to Magda, Mom?"

"She gave her the day off so we could talk," I said. "I hope you're hungry. We ordered enough for an army."

Diana frowned. "She's exaggerating. We ordered enough for two women and one hungry man. One of your brothers could easily polish off everything."

Okay, I had to meet these brothers of his. Or at least get a good look at a current photo of them. I already had a healthy respect for their appetites.

"What brings you to town, Mom? Everything all right? I didn't think anything could pry you away from those hot, young rugby players."

"Don't let your dad hear you talk like that!" She laughed. "He'll never let me manage another men's tourney again." Diana walked arm in arm with Jus to the table.

"I was talking about my brothers." He winked at her.

She laughed, a deep, rich laugh of genuine delight. She was looking at him, taking him in almost as if she was seeing him for the first time. "You've *finally* trimmed your beard. Cut your hair. And look at those clothes. You look nice." She sounded surprised. And like she didn't quite believe her eyes.

It was clear to me she considered Jus her least attractive son and was seeing him with fresh eyes. And yes, I understood the temptation. It came from knowing him too long before he'd blossomed. Of being used to overlooking the potential that had been realized, to a large extent, now. But if you looked at him, closely, as I was now, as if you were seeing him for the very first time, he was like his mom. Not handsome in the usual sense, but interesting to look at. And not in an unpleasant way. I think she was realizing that her youngest son was attractive, too.

"You can thank Kayla for my transformation, Mom." He smiled at me as I got our dinner out of the oven where it was warming.

"Changing my son already?" Her question was as pointed as a sharp stick and barbed with accusation.

"Only in superficial things like outward appearance. I've just given him a little polish." I stopped what I was doing and walked over to take his face in my hands. "Look at him. He's got fabulous bone structure. Strong, high cheekbones. Beautiful eyes. A good nose.

He's gorgeous." I smiled into his eyes, seeing myself reflected. Seeing gratitude for the lie. But was it really a lie?

"In essentials, things that really matter, there's not a thing I would change about Jus. Not *one*." I kissed him lightly and turned toward the kitchen.

Diana was staring at me with grudging respect.

I'm winning her over, I thought. *But does that matter? I'm going to betray her in the end. When the year is over...she'll hate me.*

CHAPTER THREE

Justin

Mom left around nine. She had to get up early for her return flight to Italy in the morning. Kayla and I cleaned up the dishes together. She still wasn't used to leaving things for Magda. Afterward, Kay collapsed in the sectional sofa with the Flashionista mailer in her hand.

I took a seat next to her. "Thanks for this evening. I think we did it. We convinced Mom we're the real thing."

She looked at me and smiled in a way that made my pulse race. "She's a sucker."

"Yeah? I think we're just good." I laughed to cover the fact that I hadn't been acting.

"Maybe too good." She frowned. "I think she sort of likes me."

"You sound surprised. Who wouldn't love you?"

She laughed and bumped me with her shoulder. "It's against her better judgment. Because I am obviously only out for your money." She paused. "Do you ever feel like we're getting in deeper and deeper? Like we're hurting more and more people?"

My heart thudded to a halt. It was almost like she'd read my mind. I'd been wondering all evening whether I should tell her about that text. Now was not the time. "No. We have to do what we have to do. I still don't understand why Mom changed her mind and hopped on a plane home. It's not like her."

Kayla looked at me with wide eyes and laughed. "You are *so* naïve. Entertaining her and being grilled by her was horrible. But I'm relieved she came. What mother would have absolutely *no* curiosity about her son's new wife? No, she got you with the surprise attack, Jus. She wanted to meet me when my defenses were down and you weren't around to defend me. She's smart."

"I don't get women." I put my arm over the back of the sofa.

"But you should understand moms. It's not that hard. The good ones protect their babies to the end."

"I'm not a baby."

"You'll *always* be her baby." Kayla pulled the thong and cami from the envelope almost reverently.

She was hellbent on tormenting me. I watched, mesmerized as she caressed the smooth fabric between her fingers. Imagining her caressing me like that. Damn, I was a desperate man. Watching her, and thinking of her in those panties, was turning me on.

She was having the opposite reaction to this gag gift that I had expected.

She pulled the cami out and looked at the tag. "Your staff is awesome. These are both exactly my size." She looked me in the eye. "I love this brand! They're a highly coveted boutique company. They make some of the most expensive satin and lace lingerie in the business. A set like this can easily run nearly a thousand dollars. Your employees must really love you. And that cake, from one of the most exclusive bakeries in town?"

I hated to burst her bubble. "Kay, the lingerie was a sample they pulled from our stores. The manufacturer donated it to us for our monthly sample sale because they didn't want it back. And would rather we sell it and use the money to support our charity. And the cake, we get all our cakes from them. They're just down the street from us. The owner is a good friend of Riggins'. I'm sure they gave them a discount."

She frowned as if I didn't understand the point she was making. "I understand about samples, but *still*."

I shouldn't have dispelled her illusions. "If it makes you feel any better, I'll make sure there's something of equal value in the next sample sale, if I have to buy it myself."

She turned her eyes to me. "I've heard rumors about the fabulous Flashionista sample sales. And been salivating to go to one. Don't you have to be an employee, or friends and family?" She winked at me. "Think they'll let me into one now that I'm the boss' wife?"

"I'll make sure you get in first. New rule."

"You will not! Then they'll really hate me." She held the panties up. "Your people *do* love you. Whichever merch buyer was in charge of this until the sample sale was most definitely eyeing it for herself. Believe me, there are a bunch of disappointed girls tonight." She sighed. "For so many reasons. Not the least of which is their billionaire boss is off the market." She winked at me. "They don't know it's only temporary."

She jumped up suddenly. "I'm going to try these on."

I caught her hand. "Wait just a minute. Those belong to me."

"They're for your wife."

"They're to make *me* happy." I paused for dramatic effect. "Are you going to make me happy?"

"Depends on how you define happy." She shook the mailer. "This is a community property state. Anything we acquire after the wedding, I own half of. I'm trying my half on. What do you want—tops or bottoms?"

"We have an agreement. Flashionista and my assets are excluded in the post-nup." I tightened my grip on her wrist.

"It didn't say anything about lingerie." Her eyes were alight with teasing and flirtation.

Kay had always been a flirt. It didn't mean anything. I'd seen the way she'd flirted with Lazer last night. She couldn't turn it off. Not even with me. Damn. If only it did mean something.

"A loophole! Damn that Harry for not catching it. I'll have to talk to him about it. Ask him for an addendum."

"No addendums. That wasn't part of the deal. I won't sign one." She leaned into me until her face was inches from mine. "Which half do you want?"

"That's no way to negotiate, Kay. If you want me to give on something, you have to give me something I want."

"You're willing to negotiate?"

"Make me an offer and I'll consider it."

"Make a demand and I'll counter."

"Model the underwear for me and they're all yours. Both pieces."

"You want to see me in this skimpy underwear?"

"We're man and wife. I have a right to see your naked body. I'm only asking for a partial exercise of my marital rights—to see your skimpily clad body."

She laughed. "You're the one who agreed to no sex. This is a business and friend relationship." Her voice was full of teasing. She was enjoying our exchange.

"Sure. Yeah. I agreed to no *sex*." I emphasized the word on purpose. I had sex on the brain. Every night I lay wide awake next to her, itching to touch her, frustrated out of my mind.

If I was going to seduce her it was going to be a step at a time, until she thought it was her idea. Until she had to beg me. Until she realized she was in love with me. "I didn't say anything about no nudity. Still not interested in an addendum?"

She laughed. "You're sly, Jus. Remind me never to do business with you."

"You already did."

She shook her head and laughed again. "You make a good point, though. If we're going to live together for a year, we *should* lose our inhibitions. We share a bathroom. We share a bed. It would be a lot more convenient if we got over our shyness about our bodies around each other. Much more comfortable to be able to just stroll around naked in front of you like I did with my girlfriends at the sorority house."

"The girls at the sorority house stroll around naked? Damn! How did I miss that?"

Her laugh was infectious. "Jus, you were practically still an adolescent boy. There was no way we were letting you in on our nakedness."

"Or your wild parties." I was still holding her wrist.

She rotated as if trying to wrench free, and reached for her blouse with her free hand. "Want to see me naked now?"

"No." Shit, I was a horrible liar. I was hard at the thought. And damn uncomfortable, but I refused to squirm and rearrange. "Not now. I want to see you in that lingerie. When the guys at work tease me about it, I want to speak from experience about how great it is when I flip their shit back at them."

"Oh, Jus!" Her voice was full of delight. "I think I love you. You're taking this role so seriously!"

My heart stopped. Which, I was sure, was her intention. Kayla had always had me dancing on her string, intentionally or not.

"If I'm going to be back on the singles circuit in a year, I definitely want you bragging me up to all your buddies in the meantime." She leaned over so that her breasts were in my face, and I caught a whiff of her heated perfume. "Maybe I'll catch a billionaire for real!"

She had one for real. She just didn't realize it. Or want me. The thought of her with Lazer or Riggins made my stomach burn with jealousy. Her toss-away *I love you* pierced me. Damn false hope.

She may have been playing it cool, but she was excited.

"You, my dear husband, have a deal," she whispered in my ear in a voice full of seduction.

I released her wrist, hoping I could keep my cool.

Kayla

Justin was playing with me. With him, it was hard to tell what the end game was. He was always thinking one step ahead. Was he flirting? Did he think he could get me into bed? I meant, for something other than sleeping. Was his presumed virginity making him naïve?

Casual sex was way too risky when you couldn't walk away in the morning.

But it raised the question—did I want to fall into bed with him? If the situation were different, and we'd met at a party, would I go to bed with him?

As a rebound guy, yeah, possibly. He'd be a delicious revenge on Eric. He *was* scrumptious revenge.

As I slipped into the bedroom and out of my clothes, I wondered if Jus and I would have sex at some point. Maybe to celebrate our divorce! I laughed inwardly at the ridiculousness of consummating our marriage just as we ended it.

I tossed aside my clothes and tore the tags off the fabulous lingerie. *Curses on those little plastic pieces that held the tags on.* They were almost impossible to get off without scissors.

I slipped my panties off and slid on the new thong. It fit like a dream, just a tiny triangle covering the barest essential. The cami was light pink, with lace panels strategically placed to show off my nipples. It, too, was the smoothest fabric against my skin that I'd ever felt.

I had already lost my reserve about undressing in front of the expanse of curtain-less windows. Now I marched to the mirror and studied myself. I needed one more thing. I went to the closet and got out a pair of killer stiletto heels. If I was going to strut in front of Jus to prove I had no inhibitions, I was going to really strut. As if I were on the catwalk.

I grabbed a brush and touched up my hair. Took a deep breath. Opened the bedroom door. And strutted into the living room with my hand on my hip. I'd modeled in a few charity fashion shows in college. It was amateur stuff all the girls did. It was enough to help me now.

Jus lounged on the sofa, checking his phone.

I cleared my throat.

He looked up. His eyes dilated and became round and dark. Aroused.

"Well? What do you think? Does it fit?" I stuck my hip out in the model's pose and pursed my lips into a provocative pout.

"Front looks fine. I can't believe we had this on the website. I hope we blurred out the nipples." His voice was low and sexy. His gaze fascinated with my chest. But there was still a hint of teasing in his voice.

When a guy stared at your breasts, it was hard not to bud up. It was an automatic reaction. "You should really pay more attention to your catalog. You had it on a mannequin."

"Good. We're a family-friendly site." His expression turned serious like he was concentrating. He studied me like he was evaluating whether his buyers had good taste and whether the Flash should carry more of the same type of skimpy lingerie. "Let me see the back." He twirled his finger. "Turn around."

"You just want to see my bare butt cheeks," I teased.

"I just want to see the fit."

Liar.

I turned my back to him.

"Nice ass," he said.

I looked over my shoulder at him. "You're not supposed to be looking at my ass. You promised to admire the panties. How do they look?" I wiggled my butt at him.

"No idea. I can't see them. They disappear."

"Must be a good fit, then." I smiled seductively. "I'll tell you this—they feel good. They're so comfortable. They're like wearing *nothing* at all."

"Good product? Great. I'll let the buyer know. We should offer this brand again."

He was pretending to be all business, but his voice was husky.

"Satisfied?" I asked.

He nodded. "Requirement met."

"Good. Because I'm not." I turned around to face him. "Take your shirt off."

"What?" He looked startled, but a challenge rose in his eyes and he set his jaw. "That wasn't part of the deal."

"Fair's fair, Jus. When my friends ask how hot you are, I want to be able to give them an accurate description." I flipped my hand, motioning for him to take it off. "Don't be shy."

"Damn you, Kay." But he laughed, stood, and, holding my gaze, unbuttoned his shirt, stripped it off, and dropped it on the sofa.

It was my turn to twirl my finger and command him to turn around. He complied without a word. Once his back was to me, he lifted his arms and flexed, exposing perfectly sculpted biceps and a wonderfully toned back. The man was a perfect triangle—broad shoulders tapering to a small waist. A tat covered his left shoulder.

I walked up behind him, stopping only inches from him. I used the tip of my fingernail and traced his tat until he shuddered beneath my touch. The tat hid a deep scar, the edges of which were worked into the design. "When did you get this?"

"After I left college. The guys and I all got tats together."

"No, I meant the scar."

He shrugged. "Some childhood accident. It's just one of many. I was a clumsy kid."

I leaned over and whispered into his ear. "Don't lie to me, Jus. You have to trust me. I spent several hours listening to your mom tell stories about you and your childhood. Despite what it looked like, she and I kind of bonded. I know how much you were bullied. I'd like to beat the crap out of whoever did this to you."

"I can handle myself. I fight my own battles. They paid," he said to me over his shoulder, his voice tight. "I wasn't strong. But I was fast. And cunning." His eyes glittered. He was perfectly serious. "Don't feel sorry for me, Kay. Everyone always feels sorry for me. Pity the other guy. I wasn't good with my fists, but I knew how to fight. And I played dirty."

I had never seen this side of Jus. It sent a chill down my spine. "Good, then." I paused. "Do you still play dirty?"

"When I have to." He paused. The muscles in his back tensed. It was as if he was tightly coiled. "I get what I want, Kayla. I *always* get what I want."

I shivered at the thought. There was a hint of a bad boy in this sweet, little nerd who'd blossomed into a hot guy with a to-die-for voice. For some reason, that both frightened me and turned me on. I leaned into him just close enough so the tips of my breasts brushed his hard back. "I'll have to remember not to get on your bad side, then."

I stepped back from him and turned and walked away. I knew he was watching me. I felt his gaze on me.

I swung my hips, doing the catwalk walk again. But I felt breathless.

In the bedroom, I closed the door and leaned against it. What was going on between us? When I slipped out of the thong panties, they were wet.

Justin

Kayla came out of the bedroom dressed in one of my T-shirts and a pair of cotton boxer pajama shorts, clearly signaling no sex was going down between us tonight.

"I'm going to bed." She grabbed my face, tipped it up, and, to my surprise, pressed a light kiss to my lips.

"What was that for? There's no one here." I searched her face for some clue to whether she was teasing me again.

She shrugged. "Method acting. My parents always kiss each other goodnight."

I squeezed her hand. "Goodnight, Kay. Sweet dreams."

She smiled and walked away. I watched Kayla until she disappeared. Then I sat on the couch until I was sure she was in bed, waiting until I was confident she'd had time to fall asleep. For the record, my parents didn't kiss each other goodnight. There was no way in hell I was telling Kay that. I enjoyed that tiny peck way too much. As desperate as I was, it might even become the highlight of my day.

How was I going to survive the year? At the private conference Harry and I had at the divorce meeting, he'd asked me, "Why a year, Justin?"

Why? Three main reasons. I'd only given him one—there was something about giving anything a year that was entirely respectable. If you took a new job and hated it, but stuck with it a year, you could move on without a future employer questioning why you left so soon. Without them thinking you're flaky and uncommitted. *Hey, he gave it a year. How many pounds of flesh do you want?*

Leases ran a year. School ran in years. Give anything a year and that was giving it a decent try. You were a hero.

The second reason, that I wouldn't tell him, or anyone, was simple—I figured I needed a year to catch that identity-theft bitch who'd duped me in Reno. I wasn't made a fool of lightly. Billions were at stake here. Sending me a text message had been that thief's first, and possibly fatal, mistake.

It came from a burner phone. So she wasn't totally stupid. She wanted something. Money was the logical assumption. And plenty of it. The threat of blackmail hung in the air, as close and dense as fog.

Since Saturday morning, I'd been racking my brain, trying to remember anything at all about that fateful night and the loss of my bachelorhood. Most of it was a blank. Bits and pieces were slowly coming back. Some on their own. Some with the aid of the private investigator I had secretly working for me. He uncovered little things that helped jog it.

Harry knew about the PI. Kayla hadn't asked, and I hadn't told her that I was still employing him. I was going to bring that identity-stealing bitch down. Silence her forever.

Until that text, I'd held out a small, irrational hope that I'd somehow married the real Kayla. As if she'd been mistaken about spending the night hugging the toilet. Or was lying to cover her mistake. The thought was no balm on my wounded vanity. But it would have made life simpler. Kayla, obviously, didn't want to bilk me out of my billions. She wouldn't take a hundred-thousand-dollar ring, even when I begged her and told her it would help my reputation.

I fantasized about having met up with her later that night, when she finally realized she was crazy for me after all. Yeah, me, the guy who sweeps girls off their feet with his sheer animal magnetism. I was confusing myself with one of my brothers. In my fantasies, being stood up by her was all a misunderstanding. She was too embarrassed, or too drunk, to remember it. That she was covering. That there was no crazy, criminal third party to deal with. Though that didn't say much for my prowess and magnetic sex appeal, did it? So much for false hopes and crazy fantasies.

There was another thing, something that Kayla had reinforced since we'd reconnected—she wouldn't have left me without a word. Or at least a note.

My memories of the event began with seeing Kay in the hotel lobby just after lunch last Friday. My heart lurched, like old times, at the sight of her. As much as I wanted to deny it, she still made my blood run hot. There was a part of me that wanted to show her what a big man I'd become. Not only physically. I was a frigging billionaire. I wanted to show off. I still had her number. So what the hell? Very few women could resist me now that I was a billionaire.

I texted her, asking her for a drink. Two old friends catching up. No big deal in case she shot me down. Old insecurities died hard.

Like a balm on my vanity, she texted back immediately. As if her thumbs couldn't fly fast enough to type a message back to me. She was impressed. Clearly. And I was high on it.

She asked me to meet her at a bar up the street. She specified the time, seven p.m. Thinking back, I'd been euphoric. I was no longer the scrawny kid she remembered from college. I even fixed up. Combed my beard. Put on a decent shirt and some cologne. I waited, eagerly, impatient for her to show up. The minutes ticked by. Kay wasn't usually late. She didn't power-trip on guys like that, by making them sweat waiting for her.

I was sitting alone at the bar, looking for a table to open up. A blond woman took the stool next to me. My memories of her were hazy. She reminded me of Kay, in a cheap, gauzy way. I could almost still smell her overpowering perfume. My stomach clenched.

As hard as I tried, I couldn't conjure up a clear image of her face. Maybe I'd intentionally tried to forget her. It was clear now that her similarity to Kay had been intentional. She'd set out to con me.

I clenched my jaw, suppressing my growing anger. How much did she know about Kay from her phone? What the hell had Kay stored on it? What could her impersonator use against her and us? Kayla seemed unconcerned. But shit, that woman had had her phone for hours.

I stared at the phone in my hand, wishing I'd been able to get my hands on it earlier. My pulsed quickened at the thought of dissecting this thing. I hoped to see that imposter bitch's prints on it somehow. If not literally, then figuratively. Digitally.

I'd already had Magda bag up everything I'd taken with me on my trip and give it to the PI to dust for prints. So far, nothing.

Had the ID thief worked alone? Did she have an even greedier, more dangerous partner? Whatever the case, she was the only one who would have known to send that threatening text. I had to find her. Shut her down and keep her from talking.

First, I had to string her along as long as I could. I had to erase any evidence of marrying a phony. Any evidence that the girl I'd married wasn't the sweet, beautiful girl in my bed. The one I could barely keep my hands off.

I had to be sure there was no photographic or video evidence. No surveillance video of us anywhere. No way anyone could prove I hadn't married the real Kayla. I was reasonably certain my little thief was savvy enough to avoid as many cameras as possible. She was undoubtedly a professional. She would have kept her face hidden from the cameras.

Storing surveillance video for more than thirty to sixty days, ninety at most, was prohibitively expensive. I had to keep this under wraps for a *minimum* of thirty days. String her along if I had to. Ninety days and I would be golden. Totally in the clear. Any surveillance video would be overwritten by then. No business stored it longer than that. Then it would just be Kay's word and mine against this whore's. I hoped that ID thief didn't realize the same thing. Just what kind of IQ was I dealing with? Not a genius. She'd already screwed up.

But then, so had I.

I shuddered. Just what the hell had I done with that woman? Had I slept with her? Was she laughing at my inexperience? Should I be checked for sexually transmitted diseases? Would she suddenly reappear claiming to be pregnant with my baby?

Another month and I would be in the clear there, too.

The thought of her being pregnant with my kid made me sick. I leaned forward and put my head in my hand. She had to know that was a crazy plan. I would insist on a paternity test. Use every resource I had against her. She'd have to be insane to sleep with marks and not use birth control. Unless she'd known who I was. Then she might have tried to get pregnant. But that didn't seem like her MO.

If she'd wanted to catch me with a baby, why hadn't she stuck around? Why hadn't she married me under her real name? No, she had to have seen the news and realized her mistake in letting a big fish get away.

I kept thinking, I kept hoping, she'd just wanted to get into my room that night and steal what she could. She'd lifted ten thousand dollars from me. Money I'd won in the casino. I had a very good memory. I could count cards and read faces. Spot a tell a mile away. If the casinos knew, they would ban me. So I always played it carefully, losing a few times on purpose, and not getting greedy. Gambling was fun sport for me. I didn't want to lose the ability to play now and again.

Stealing from me? Whatever. Ten grand was chump change to me now. It was more the humiliation, being played for a fool, that sent me into a dangerous slow burn. I'd been bullied too much of my life to put up with any shit now. This bitch wasn't going to get away with pushing me around and trying to take my money. She wasn't smart enough to fool me again.

I wished I could remember something more. If the money hadn't been missing, I wouldn't have even been certain she'd been in my room.

There was another thing I was pretty sure of—she'd drugged my drink. I had all the classic symptoms, including memory loss.

How many other people had she tricked and stolen from? I had to find this woman. She had to have an online presence. I wasn't giving up until I found her. And then...I would put a stop to her.

I took a deep breath and stood. My home office had a secure server. Whatever I did there would be private. No one would know what I was up to. I would recognize the woman if I saw her again.

I took a deep breath and tried to think. I remembered flashes going off in the bar. People snapping pictures. There was a chance I'd accidentally photobombed someone's picture. And another smaller chance they'd caught both me and the woman in the same shot. With a clear enough view of her face to identify her.

And posted the picture online somewhere. Okay, very long odds. But I was desperate.

My pulse raced as I thought through the implications. I calmed down as I realized that a picture of a girl and me sitting next to each other in a bar didn't prove I'd married her. She couldn't use that to convict me.

I would use my picture and facial-recognition software and see what I could find. If I could get a clear enough picture of her, I could use the same facial-recognition software to find her. I *was* going to find her. If I had to scour the entire Internet.

And when I did...

I turned my attention to Kay's phone.

CHAPTER FOUR

Kayla

I woke up at three a.m., cold from the blasting air conditioning, startled to see Jus in bed next to me. For an instant, before I spotted the beard, I thought he was Eric. It was almost instinctive to curl up to him for warmth. And yet part of me knew I was mad at Eric and he shouldn't be next to me in bed. I stopped myself just in time, temporarily confused. It was like that feeling you have sometimes when you're on vacation and you wake up in a strange room. And it takes you a sec to remember where you are. Now add in strange room *and* strange guy.

It took me a second to wake up enough to remember I was married. To Jus. I was startled as I realized I wasn't as disappointed that he wasn't Eric as I should have been. I'd spent the last six years thinking Eric was the love of my life. It was odd, but being with Justin was almost comforting.

His face was relaxed in sleep. He slept with his arm over his head. And his phone on the mattress between us? I did a double take. That was carrying staying connected a little too far. I leaned over and suppressed a laugh. Jus was running one of those sleep apps. He was such a data nerd.

His breathing was slow and even, not at all gasping, like I'd heard people with sleep apnea do. And he didn't snore. Why did he need this data?

The bed was big. Jus had been keeping to his own side. I slid closer to him and stealthily picked up the phone. What would it hurt to have a little fun with him? I shook the phone several times before returning it and sliding back to my side. Jus was a sound sleeper. He didn't even stir.

In the meantime, I was still cold. His bed had every amenity, including temperature control. I hadn't bothered learning how to operate it. I made a mental note to give it a try in the morning. To set the firmness of my mattress. My angle of repose. And the temperature, which I could set to come on and warm up the bed so it would be all cozy at bedtime. Since when had beds become so complicated?

I sighed and fell back on my pillow. Every aspect of life with a billionaire was complicated. I didn't remember falling asleep, but when I woke up, Jus and his phone were already gone.

I got up, showered, dressed, and checked my phone out of habit. Two messages. First one from Jus: *At work. Didn't want to wake you when I left, sleepyhead. Left an envelope with some cash and ideas about a household/personal budget with Magda. We need to take care of some administrative things. Talk tonight. Have a good day. I love you, babe.*

Babe? Did I hear sarcasm in that? He was taking this fakery to a whole new level by infiltrating my phone with sweet gushiness and ordinary, mundane domestic life details. And professions of love. Then again, it was probably smart and added authenticity to our deception. If a court ever subpoenaed my phone, we were good.

He had a good point—I needed a budget. Billionaire's wives didn't go around dressed in cheap clothes without a penny to their names. How was I supposed to jet-set without working capital?

I texted him back. *I love you more! Miss you already! Have the best day ever, sweetie. XOXO*

I added a pair of kissy lips and three emoticon hearts and smirked at the utter junior highness of it. Jus would get the humor. I wondered if we could work out a code using hearts and sweet nothings. I laughed at the idea of my phone being full of beautiful love messages that really meant things like *Pick up a loaf of bread on your way home.*

The second message was from Brittany. *Free for lunch? You'd better be! Meet me at noon at...* She named one of our favorite restaurants near where she worked downtown. It would be crowded with her coworkers at lunch, but that was life.

I knew what she wanted—details. Ordinarily I would have jumped at the chance to lunch with her. Don't get me wrong. I wanted to see her. I just wasn't certain I was ready. Then again, there was that old saying, *There's no time like the present.* I was going to have to face her eventually. I texted back that I'd be there.

When I came out of the bedroom, Magda was banging around in the kitchen. Jus had been up late in his office. I was naturally curious about what he'd been doing in there. I had my suspicions. I hadn't been home much in our two days of married life, but when I was, the door was closed. Which, of course, made it all the more intriguing. What was he hiding in there? It was the one room he'd barely given me a glimpse of. It was closed this morning, too.

Magda smiled at me. "Mrs. Kayla, what can I get you?"

I hesitated. I wasn't used to being waited on. And though it was supposedly the most important meal of the day, I generally dashed off without eating breakfast. "Coffee. Caramel or hazelnut. Something flavored. And frothed milk and sugar. A piece of toast, maybe?"

She rattled off a selection of breads that would have given a restaurant a five-star rating.

"Whole wheat." I was trying to be healthy.

"Mr. Justin left an envelope for you on the counter." She pointed, ground her coffee fresh, sliced a hunk of bread, and popped it in the toaster.

I grabbed the envelope and tried not to gasp when I glanced inside and saw a thousand dollars in cash and a shiny new credit card. Not a black card, unfortunately. Jus evidently thought I needed a much lower credit limit. Maybe he was right to be cautious, haha. There was a sticky note attached to the credit card: *I added you to this account.*

It was written in block letter print, like engineers use. Fairly neat. Legible, which was all that mattered. The sight of it made my pulse race and brought a smile to my face. There was something about Jus...

The toast popped up. Magda buttered it and set it before me on the counter along with a crystal bowl of fresh, homemade strawberry jam.

"Mr. Justin said strawberry is your favorite. The strawberry crop is good this year. I just made a large batch last week. Now that I know this, I'll make another this afternoon." Magda set a cup of coffee in front of me while I marveled that Jus remembered I loved strawberries, and strawberry jam was an absolute weakness of mine.

"Speaking of Mr. Justin," Magda said, "you need to take better care of him."

I looked at her, startled. Magda apparently held an old-fashioned view of marriage. Like somehow Jus was my charge. "How so?"

"He left the house wearing that ugly brown shirt of his and the greenish jeans he likes. It doesn't go together. Mr. Justin has no sense of color. I can't argue him out of wearing those colors together. Believe me, I've tried. He gets defensive. I know my place and value my job, so I keep my mouth shut now." She gave me a sly look. "You have more pull with him and a good sense of style."

She was obviously offering the olive branch, bonding with me by worrying over how Jus dressed and looked. She was so cute, almost motherly in her concern for his image.

"I can't change him." I meant it.

She arched an eyebrow.

I laughed. "*Much*. He was wearing mismatched colors?" I frowned.

"Yes, and after he looked so nice yesterday when you dressed him." She sighed. "You know what I think? I'm tempted to sew little tags in his clothes so he knows what goes with what. Like that children's clothing line from years ago when mine were small." She chuckled.

I didn't exactly dress him. An image flashed through my mind. Sliding an expensive, perfectly tailored shirt over his broad shoulders. I knew exactly the cut. Round armholes instead of the standard oval, for a slimmer fit across the chest. Buttoning mother-of-pearl buttons one by one up his hard chest. Lingering just enough to touch and tease him. An "accidental" touch here and there. Zipping the fly of handsewn slacks...

I felt myself flush. Great clothes and a good body were my weakness...

"It will be bad for his new image, and yours, if you let him slip out like that again." She sighed heavily.

Magda startled me out of my fantasy. Her tone was scolding. Clearly she thought I needed to get up and see him off properly. To take care of my guy. Living in a sorority house had taught me many things. Rule number one—never alienate the help. I needed Magda on my side.

"You're right!" I smiled at her. "We can't let him go out looking like...usual."

She smiled, pleased and satisfied with herself, as she nodded. "His business is known for its fashion and flair, and there is Mr. Justin in his sad, mismatching colors..." She shook her head.

Obviously unfashionable. I flashed her a conspiratorial smile, knowing full well I was being manipulated.

"You've shown me the light, Magda. Attacking his closet and, for lack of a better word, streamlining his wardrobe is now a priority on my list of things to do."

"You should go shopping for him, too." She busied herself wiping down the milk frother, tossing the comment off nearly under her breath.

She was good.

"I should go shopping for him," I said, as if it was all my idea. "Fun!"

"It will be a nice break from all the paperwork to change your name." She gave me a smile of complete sympathy.

I froze. "I—"

She waved a hand at me. "No one looks forward to it. I have seven nieces. One of them has been married three times. Changing your driver's license, your social security card, your passport, it's all a pain in the ass." She nodded. "But worth it, completely worth it in the end. The name Green carries weight. Opens doors. Mrs. Justin Green means something in this town. Any woman would be proud to take it." She puffed up her chest.

Magda was barrel-chested to begin with. I almost laughed at her puffery. She had a good point. I'd been so shocked at being married, I'd wanted to keep my name almost as a reflex. As if I needed to hang on to my identity. Only a few days in, though, she had me rethinking things. Damn! That woman was a master manipulator. A shiver slid down my back. Had she been a fly on the wall and heard me tell Jus as part of our agreement I didn't want to change my name?

"Um, yes." How erudite of me.

"You should get on it right away. No use putting it off. It doesn't get any easier. Dealing with government offices never does. The sooner you're officially Mrs. Green, the better for you."

Yes, she was right! Crap, she really had a good point.

Two could play the manipulation game. I wanted in to Justin's office, and she was my ticket. "Yes, you're right. I should tackle that after lunch. I'll be out for lunch. I'm meeting a friend."

She nodded.

"I'll need our marriage license, won't I? I think I left it in Justin's office."

I felt her watching me as I walked across the room and tried his office door. "It's locked."

She shrugged. She wasn't surprised. "It's always locked."

"You must have the key." Housekeepers always had the key.

She shook her head. "Sadly, no."

"But how do you clean in there if you can't get in?"

She wrinkled her nose. "I don't. He has valuable, delicate equipment in there. He doesn't like *anyone* touching it. Not even to dust it."

So. A mystery. What was Jus hiding in there?

Magda smiled like she had my number. "Good news, though. I know where the license is, and it isn't locked up!" She opened a cupboard in the kitchen and pulled out an envelope. "He keeps his bills and important papers here." She handed me the license.

I took it back to my bedroom and held it in my shaking hands while I stared at the signature. It looked nearly identical to mine. Would it fool a handwriting expert, though? I wondered whether I should start trying to copy this fake.

I met Brittany at a combination pizza and biscuit place near the corporate campus where she worked. The restaurant concept sounded weird, but basically it was two restaurants in one. You could go to the biscuit half and get a biscuit topped with just about anything. Gravy. Ham and cheese. Fruit. You name it. Or the pizza half and have one of the best, and most unusual, pizzas in town. The place, as always, was packed with staffers from Britt's office. The crowd was mostly our age to early thirties. Some of the brightest, most ambitious people in the city.

Britt was a merch buyer for one of the world's largest online retailers. Housewares. They paid well, but they were demanding. You either performed or you were fired. A-minus performance was unacceptable. Every year after performance reviews, the lowest-rated workers were let go.

Britt had already lasted three years. The company had once been known for its innovative startup environment. That had faded before Britt joined. Now they were becoming mired in established business mentality. It wore on Britt. And housewares weren't really her thing. Like me, she was dying to get her hands on a young, trendy designer fashion brand. Both of us had majored in fashion merchandising in college, though at different universities. Rival cross-state universities. Somehow our friendship had survived it.

Britt was waiting for me. She had managed to grab a small table off the main aisle. She waved to me. I waved back and waded through the crowd to her. When I got to the table, she jumped up and hugged me with exuberance reserved for major happy life news.

"Look at you!" She held me at arm's length, studying me closely. "The beautiful new bride!"

I laughed. "Do I look married? That's a shame. How's life at the world's biggest store?"

"Hectic. Stressful. As always." Her smile was big. "But enough about me. Look at you! I want to know *everything*. And I mean every detail. I want the truth and nothing but." She gave me the same truth-piercing gaze she'd used since we were baby high school frosh. "First things first. Show me the ring!"

I held my left hand out and flashed Justin's Order of the Engineer ring at her as if it were a mega-carat diamond monstrosity, holding back a laugh.

"What the crap is that?" She grabbed my hand and pulled it to her face for a closer look. "Is that pot metal?"

I laughed. "Steel, I think."

She shook her head. "It goes without saying—I expected better from a billionaire. It looks like those rings engineers wear on their pinkies."

"Very astute! It's exactly that. The wedding was...impromptu. He had to improvise." I wiggled my fingers for emphasis, like I were showing off the Ashberg Diamond.

"I saw you ring shopping on the news last night." Still with the look. "Where's the real ring?"

"They're sizing it. I should get it tomorrow."

"Good! You should have it in time for the party I'm throwing for you two on Saturday."

"Saturday?"

"What, are you busy? Everyone is dying to meet the groom. I can't put them off indefinitely!"

"Saturday's great." I hoped Jus would agree.

"Good. My place." She gave me a time. "I can't wait to see the ring in person. I saw a picture of it on the news. Only twenty-five thousand? Cheapskate!" She shook her head and winked.

"I didn't say how much it cost." I gave her a pointed look. That would be gauche.

"No, but the news did." She smiled innocently.

I didn't remember giving the store permission to release the cost of the ring. But the press could have found out by any number of means.

"That's my fault. I wouldn't let him spend more. The ring is big enough as it is." I laughed. Jus had been right. People were already blaming him for being cheap.

A waiter brought me a glass of water and took my drink order.

"I already ordered our favorite pizza," Britt said. "Stupid short lunch hours. I have to make the most of every minute."

I laughed. Seeing Britt felt incredibly good.

She ogled the waiter as he disappeared. "He has a fine ass. Too bad he doesn't have a better job."

I laughed at her. "Gold digger. Social climber."

"Shut up! Look who's talking." She took a sip of water and watched me over the top of her glass. "Justin isn't here to overhear us. Spill it! How in the world did you end up married to Seattle's most eligible nerd? What were you *thinking*?" She leaned across the table to me. "Just how drunk were you, you lucky thing?"

"Lucky?"

"You're married to a billionaire! Isn't that every girl's fantasy?"

"Well—"

"It's mine." She paused, still staring me down. "Working here in the high-tech corridor, I'm hoping to run into a hot entrepreneur and take him down. And you haven't answered my question."

I sighed and went for the old partial truth form of lying that's renowned in intelligence circles the world over. "We were both pretty out of it." I went for broke.

I didn't need her prying into details of the ceremony. "Neither of us remember the ceremony very clearly."

At my frank, yet lying, admission, she nearly sputtered on her water. "Out of it? Really? Since that episode in college, you're so cautious with alcohol you're practically a non-drinker."

She was referring to a particular time when I drank one too many tequila slammers and got exceedingly sick. "I drink!" Why was I so defensive? My heart raced. I fought to keep my smile in place. "Just not tequila."

I sighed dramatically. "Blame it on Eric. He'd just dumped me for that new bitch." I didn't have to fake the venom. I leaned back, as if that explained everything.

She nodded sympathetically, but didn't look totally convinced. "But getting drunk and married on the rebound? So drunk you don't even remember the details of the ceremony?" She sighed again. She was exasperated with me, and worried. "That's taking rebounds to a whole new level. And it doesn't sound like you at all. Sure, you can throw the rich-bitch thing in Eric's face now. But..."

I knew what she meant. Had I really cut off my nose to spite my face? That's what she was asking. I couldn't set her straight. There was a price for everything. The price for helping Jus and gaining a lifetime of freedom was appearing like a vindictive, stupid bitch. Shallow. I was going to be swallowing my pride for the next year at least.

"Is Justin aware he's rebound guy?" Britt was still studying me with that look she used when she grilled me about guys.

I shrugged. There was no point in denying it. This was Britt, with her off-the-scale emotional IQ. She would snoop it out, anyway.

Her eyes narrowed. "Are you having second thoughts?"

"No!" I shook my head. "Are you kidding? Absolutely not. Jus is sweet. And committed. Which is more than I can say for Eric."

Britt nodded. "All true. But Eric is hot. *Very* hot."

"How superficial do you think I am?" I tried to look indignant. "There are more important things than looks. Looks fade."

She cocked an eyebrow. "But until they do, hot is good. And Jus is—"

"A work in progress. With potential." I grinned at her. "Come on! You saw the news. I was right, wasn't I? He *is* hotter than he looked."

Britt gave me a slow, sly smile. "*Much.* I'm relieved to see you defending him. Maybe there's hope." She looked as if she might actually believe I was attracted to him. "Jus might not be Eric, but he is striking. Is that the right word? His looks are interesting. His new look is your handiwork?"

I grinned. "I can't take credit for his growth spurt, obviously. But his new sense of fashion? Yeah. Absolutely." I grinned slyly again and tried to sell it. "He has a really hot body now, too. Also not my doing. Abs to die for."

She lifted one perfectly plucked eyebrow. "Really?"

"Oh, yeah."

"The main question is—how does he use that body? Is he good in bed?"

"Perfect," I lied. Sort of. He was fine to actually sleep with. Didn't hog the bed or anything.

She grinned. "So. How long is this marriage going to last?"

Crap. She nearly gave me heart failure. I paled. It was as if she knew the terms of our agreement. Then I realized she was just being her usual skeptical self. "We have as good a chance as any couple." In reality, 362 days left.

"A word of advice, Lala." She used my pet name that only my family used. But she was practically like a sister to me.

"I'm listening." I took a sip of water.

"Get pregnant. ASAP." Her face was set and dead serious.

"What?" I nearly spewed my water all over the table. "I'm not ready for children! We haven't even talked about them." I paused and grinned. "There wasn't a lot of time in our whirlwind four-hour romance to discuss much." I laughed, trying to make light.

She shook her head, looking at me suspiciously. "Lala, you were always the nice, responsible voice of reason. I'm having a hard time digesting this sudden marriage of yours. It doesn't make sense."

"I already told you. One word—Eric." I raised an eyebrow. "He makes me do crazy crap. This may be the best mistake I've ever made." Or the worst. The jury was still out.

She played with her fork. "You're evading the issue again. Don't *talk* to Justin about kids. Just flush your pill down the toilet each day and get pregnant. Once you have his kid—you only need one—you're set for life."

"I can't believe you! I had no idea you were this cynical and mercenary!" I was only half kidding. I was shocked, though I probably shouldn't have been. Britt had always been practical and pragmatic about life. She'd been called an opportunist more than once.

Britt set the fork down. Her face was serious. "Not mercenary. *Practical.* You two got married for all the wrong reasons. And you know it."

That was true enough.

"You got drunk and he got horny. You were...well...we already discussed what you were. Sad. Depressed. Out to make a point to Eric. You didn't think anything through. Jus is young. Beneath that beard he probably still looks twelve. He's also a billionaire. Which makes him desirable no matter what he looks or acts like. Enough said. This *won't* last."

I was insulted. It was irrational. But it was what it was. I opened my mouth to protest.

She cut me off. "Don't bother arguing. I *hope* it lasts. But odds are it won't. You need to be smart about this and protect yourself. Get yourself a little bundle of baby insurance. You won't get another chance like this again."

I frowned, more upset than I liked to admit. She didn't know the terms of our agreement. When I left the marriage with "only" ten million, she would think I'd been screwed. And I could never set her straight.

"I haven't even changed my name yet and you're telling me to get pregnant!" I laughed, almost nervously. Britt knew me better than anyone, and I had the feeling she was seeing right through me. "My housekeeper thinks I'm out taking care of the name change this afternoon." I laughed like that was funny. "Jus said I could keep my maiden name."

Britt was going to get frown lines if she kept staring at me with that expression. "Don't even. Your housekeeper is right. Change your name immediately, the minute you leave this lunch. Integrate yourself into Justin's life as deeply as possible. Make it near to impossible for him to get you out of it. Change it this afternoon without telling him."

"I like my name."

She shook her head, as if I was being naïve. "Justin has been in love with you since he first saw you. I'm not terribly surprised he proposed marriage hours after seeing you again, even if he was totally drunk. It's you who I'm puzzled by. That damn Eric.

"Anyway, back to business. Change your name to Justin's now, while he's in the honeymoon phase. Do it as a surprise. If the past is any indication, he'll be ridiculously pleased you took his name. Most guys are. Deep down they like to caveman it and believe you're their woman. They like the idea of ownership.

"Surprise him with the news tonight over a bottle of his favorite alcoholic beverage. Get him drunk again and make that baby you need." Her eyes danced. "Trust me on this one, Lala. I only have your best interests at heart.

"Oh, and while you're at it, sweet-talk him into making me a senior merch buyer at Flashionista. I've been dying to get in there. Half my team has abandoned me for the Flash, as they call it. They're ridiculously happy working for Justin. The Flash still has that innovative, fun startup vibe. We used to have it. But that was before my time. I'm dying to get out of the corporate atmosphere."

I rolled my eyes. "You're pimping me out for a job? Some friend! You could just apply."

"Is it pimping someone out when you ask them to sleep with their husband?" She winked. "The Flash is growing. But they're recruiting entry level. I should have gotten in earlier. I need a senior position." She smiled sweetly at me. "Friend, what do you say? You own half that company now."

I laughed. "Hardly!"

She looked at me, puzzled. "Come on! Don't give me some crap about a prenup. There couldn't have been time to sign one. They don't offer legal services at twenty-four-hour chapels now, do they?"

I'd almost messed up again! "Jus doesn't own the *whole* company. He has a partner and a boatload of shareholders. But I'll see what I can do."

She smiled. "Good! I've heard Justin and his partner Riggins are dreams to work for." She leaned across the table toward me. "I probably shouldn't tell you this, but my former colleagues who work for the Flash call Justin the cute billionaire." She nodded, looking like she enjoyed my shock.

"Of course they do! He's adorable," I said. And he was. Truly.

"When your marriage was announced, there were a lot of devastated girls at the Flash," she said with a twinkle in her eyes. "If you want to keep him, watch your husband and keep him happy. A little thing like a quickie wedding won't stop some of those girls.

"That's another thing. Keep an eye on Flashionista. Take an active interest in it. It's right up your alley. Make yourself invaluable to the business. Don't make the mistake of ignoring your husband's business and being dumb about where he keeps his assets. Find out where he banks and where he stashes his investments. Be smart about this, Lala."

The waiter interrupted by serving our pizza. I was salivating over it and reaching for a pizza plate, totally distracted by thoughts of food, when I caught the silhouette of a man out of the corner of my eye. And caught a whiff of cologne I would recognize anywhere.

The man and that sexy cologne stopped at our table. "Kayla?"

I looked up into the devastatingly handsome face of Lazer Grayson.

CHAPTER FIVE

Kayla

My heart pounded. My pulse raced. My world lit up. If my life had been a movie, I would have started dancing and singing. Instead I stood and hugged him. "Lazer!"

He smiled into my eyes. His hands went to my waist. Friendly. Intimate. On the edge of decorum. And positively thrilling. I felt them as if they scorched. His face was inches from mine. Up close, his eyes were dark and dazzling. His smoothly shaved face sensual and crying out to be touched. I had to bunch my fist to resist stroking his cheeks.

He was dressed in a custom-made suit with lines so classic and simple it had to have cost thousands. The fabric was fine, soft high quality beneath my fingers. The way it moved was pure poetry written in summer wool. The shirt beneath the suit coat tapered to show off his trim abs and waist in a classic Italian silhouette. The buttons were mother-of-pearl and handsewn in invisible stitching, a hallmark of a certain Italian designer. He looked as if he'd just stepped out of a men's fashion shoot. He rattled me in ways I didn't want to admit to. I could barely think.

"Funny running into you here, princess-maker." I felt intoxicated and breathless in his presence.

His eyes danced. He seemed charmed that I was flirting with him. "They're working on it. You got your nondisclosure? I haven't seen you online playing."

My pulse fluttered. My heart and ego danced. He'd been watching for me online! "Not yet. I thought you got busy and forgot all about me." I couldn't have been more obvious if I'd batted my eyes at him. I couldn't help myself.

"How could I? You and Justin have been all over the news."

Was there an edge of regret in his voice? Whatever he felt, his comment brought me back to myself and the reality of my situation. I shouldn't be flirting with him. Especially not in front of Britt. I simply smiled.

"I'll follow up this afternoon. They've been swamped. Give them a few days. If you don't get an invitation by Monday or Tuesday, text me." He leaned in and whispered, "I've missed our gaming. The red room of game hasn't been the same since you left."

His comment made me ridiculously happy. "That's only because you beat me handily. I'm glad we ran into each other. What brings you here?"

He hitched a thumb over his shoulder toward the main campus of one of Seattle's biggest businesses. "Picking up a pizza to go. I had business with the everything store. It ran into my lunch hour. Such is the life of a businessman. Always eating on the go. What are you doing here? Besides the obvious?"

Britt cleared her throat.

I blushed. I'd been so captivated by Lazer, I'd screwed up my cover in front of Britt and her watching eyes. "Oh, sorry! I'm lunching with my best friend." I stepped out of his embrace, which had lasted longer than appropriate. "Lazer, this is Britt. Britt, meet Lazer Grayson."

She was eyeing him like quarry. I felt a stab of jealousy as I realized she was free to pursue him. *And I wasn't.* At the same time, I took great joy in the shocked and awed look on her face. She knew whom Lazer was, and was impressed.

"A pleasure." She flashed him her flirty smile.

To my relief, he smiled back politely, but didn't return the flirt.

A waiter recognized him and came over, carrying a pizza box. "Mr. Grayson, sorry about the wait! Here's your pie."

Lazer thanked the waiter, took his pizza, and flashed me a look of regret. "I have to run. I'll be in touch as soon as your princess is done. I want your approval before we release her into the wilds of the gaming world. We'll catch up soon! Promise." He winked and left me standing at the table, drooling after him.

"What is *going on* between you two?"

I jumped at the sound of Britt's voice, realizing I was still standing when I should have been sitting. "Nothing. He's a friend of Justin's."

"Whoa. Talk about animal magnetism. It fairly drips off him. No wonder he's been voted Seattle's hottest bachelor so many times." Britt's eyes became thin and suspicious. "He's making you a princess, is he?"

"In a video game."

"Yeah, I figured." She paused and studied me. "No second thoughts, huh? *Liar.*"

There are people you can fool. And people you can't. Britt was one of the latter.

"I'm not sorry I married Jus." That much was true.

She sighed. "Snap judgment here—Lazer is too much like Eric, too damned hot for his own good. And he knows it. Love is partly in the mind. Convince yourself you're in love with Jus. Tell yourself how mad about him you are at every turn.

"Make a baby with him. Before you make a fool of yourself with Lazer Grayson." She slid a slice of pizza onto a plate. "Be careful. You're playing with fire. With a man like Lazer, it's impossible not to get scorched. Although I wouldn't mind giving it a try." She flashed me a devilish grin. "Invite me and him over sometime. Soon."

Justin

I don't scare easily, not after having gone through all the shit I've been through. But I was tense as I waited for the ID thief to make her next move. My facial-recognition software had been running for over fifteen hours and come up empty. It was still early days. I would get her yet.

After fighting traffic—an accident had blocked a lane of I-90 across the lake and snarled traffic—I was home later than expected. Magda was used to leaving something warming for me in the oven.

I braced myself before letting myself into the penthouse. Yesterday I'd come home to the unpleasant surprise of Mom grilling Kay. What would I find today? Nothing short of a demonic presence would surprise me. I wanted alone time. I had a surprise for Kay burning a hole in my pocket.

When I opened the door, the table was set for two. Candles flickered. Soft music played. Something smelled delicious. There was no Mom ready to pounce. And best of all, Kay greeted me with a brilliant smile. As if she was genuinely delighted to see me. For an instant, I let myself believe she was in love with me. That this whole damned mistake had turned out to be the best thing that ever happened to me. That there was no identity thief and no Lazer with his eye on her. I almost pulled the box in my pocket out for her right then.

Before I could, her gaze ran up and down me. Her brow puckered slightly. She broke into a grin. Something about me amused her. As if there was an inside joke I was on the outside of. Yes, I was damned insecure. In business, I was completely in control. But love was another matter. I was all too aware of my inadequacies as a lover and romantic partner.

"You're home!" She slipped off the sofa and greeted me with a hug and a quick whisper of a kiss, just enough to tantalize me.

"Are we alone?" I whispered to her, the bulge in my pocket evident. I hoped she didn't feel it.

She laughed. She knew what I meant. Were we putting on a show? If we weren't, why were we kissing? Was this part of her method acting? Another routine to fall into so we looked authentic? Or was she trying to kill me?

"Completely and totally alone." She winked as she took my hand. "More method acting. I'm so afraid I'll slip out of character in public if I don't get used to playing the role twenty-four-seven. Even in private. My parents always kiss when they come home."

Mine didn't. But they usually worked together anyway. So there was my answer. Every day, I would get a quick welcome-home kiss that meant nothing more than a peck on the cheek. Every day, I would be in torment, wishing I knew how to make her fall in love with me. Wondering if a year, or a lifetime, was enough time.

She grabbed the sleeve of my shirt and playfully tugged it. "Jus," she said in an intimate, light tone that felt like a punch to the gut. I wanted her to love me so damn bad. "What is this?"

For an instant, I thought she'd spotted the box in my jeans pocket. I wasn't ready to spring it on her yet. I looked down to where her slender fingers, with their perfectly manicured nails, bright pink and expertly shaped, held my shirt. If I hadn't started Flashionista, her girly-ness would have been completely foreign to me. I grew up with two he-man brothers and a dad to match. Mom didn't care about her nails. "My favorite brown shirt."

Her eyes danced, and that smile played at the edges of her generous mouth in a way that both scared the shit out of me and brought up every insecurity I had. If she was laughing *at* me...

She grabbed the pocket of my green jeans. "And these?"

My heart raced again as I imagined her sticking her hand in and pulling out a ring box. "My green jeans."

She held my gaze and leaned into me until her breasts brushed against me. She seemed oblivious to my secret. "Jus, sweetie, I hate to break this to you, but these jeans are brown. A cool brown at that. Your shirt is a warm green. They clash, babe."

I could let her call me babe all day long. But she was wrong. "Magda's gotten hold of you and turned you against me."

I laughed, but I was irritated. I didn't give a shit about clothes. But I didn't appreciate the help turning my wife against me, either. My shirt and pants matched perfectly, color-wise. What else mattered? "She hates this outfit. I can't believe she turned you."

Kayla didn't answer. She was still staring at me, brow furrowed, eyes narrowed.

If we were going to talk about clothes, I was going to make a point, too. "And while we're talking about colors—why do you wear so much gray? You're so hot when you wear something vibrant."

She smiled slightly, cocked her head, dropped my hand, and took a step back from me. She pulled at her blouse. "You mean like this blouse?"

"Exactly like that." I nodded. "You should wear something brighter and colorful. I don't like gray."

"Jus, this is light pink." Her voice was soft. Her lips were moist and kissable. But her voice was determined and firm. "It's one of my favorite colors."

Why did everyone argue with me about colors?

When I didn't say anything, she touched my arm lightly. "What color is peanut butter?"

"That's random." I didn't get where she was going.

"It's totally pertinent. Just answer the question."

I shrugged, playing along. "It's green, of course."

"Oh, Jus," she said in that pitying tone of voice I hated.

"What?" I felt myself getting defensive.

She pulled her phone from the pocket of her jeans and looked something up. A second later, she turned the phone around, showing me a picture of a jar of peanut butter. "Read the description."

"Rich peanutty flavor, deep tan color—" I stopped. Shit. In twenty-one years no one had thought to ask me the color of peanut butter, or debate it with me. Until Kay. She paid attention to the details of me. Which was more than I could say about anyone before I became a billionaire.

I swallowed. "Okay. Point made." I tamped down my frustration. I looked like a stupid fool. All my inadequacies surfaced. I'd been laughed at all my life for the colors I chose. It had never dawned on me there might be a genetic reason I'd been slow to learn my colors. My parents took that weakness as proof I was normal. I wasn't quick at everything, thank God.

She held my gaze. "This peanut butter looks green to you?"

I nodded, wondering if her eyes were really the beautiful lilac I saw. Or her hair the shiny blond I loved.

"Do you have trouble telling the difference between stoplights and streetlights at night? Are they the same color to you?"

"Yeah. Until I get close." Everything was making sense. I felt stupid. But why would I question how I saw the world? How would I really know the green I saw wasn't the green everyone saw? Or that stoplights didn't just get their color when you were almost beneath them? Yeah, I'd always thought it was crappy design, but what else was new?

"Jus, I think you're colorblind." Her voice was soft and sympathetic. "Have you ever been tested?"

"No." I shook my head and blamed my parents, who were always too busy with my sports hero brothers.

"No one ever noticed before?" She looked incredulous.

"I've been given every damn IQ test there is. No one cares about my artistic ability. They've always thought I'm either being contrary or eccentric in my color choices. Or just slow to learn them. Or developmentally behind artistically." My words came out sounding bitterer than I intended.

"There's a very good test we can take online. We had to take it in college at the start of one of my fine arts classes. The professor actually had a fourth color receptor and saw more colors than everyone else. Millions of colors. He wanted to make sure he understood his students' capabilities and limitations. He's a wise man."

I liked the way she used we.

"We'll take the test after dinner. I'm sure it will confirm what I suspect. I'm ninety-nine percent certain you're colorblind. It will tell us what kind of colorblind you are and how severe it is."

"So I'm color challenged?" I hung my head, hamming it up and making a play for her sympathy.

"It's not a disability." She laughed and tipped my chin up. "Not really. We all live in the same world, but we all experience it differently. What most people see as brown, you see as green—and vice versa. You're right. And we're right. The key is to understand our different perceptions and accept them."

She paused and got a devilish look in her eyes. "But you *are* going to have to let me dress you. Every single day. You have a reputation to maintain, especially now. People can be cruel. I won't have anyone making fun of you."

I laughed. "Let them try! I'm a rich techie. Caring about how I look will ruin my techie rep."

She took my cheek in her hand. "No, you're my scorching-hot billionaire husband. You run the company that sets fashion trends that girls everywhere melt over. You offer them the dream of designer, boutique clothes at fantastic prices they can afford. You have to be the face, and body, of it. You're the man every guy wants to be. And don't you ever forget it."

"You're talking about my partner Riggins."

"I'm talking about you." She dropped her hand from my face. I felt the absence of her touch as an immediate loss. Kay was the only person who took the time to see and accept me. I loved her even more for that, wishing she would take her own wise words and see me as the guy who would never betray her. As the guy who would treat her right.

"I need your permission to go through your closet and organize it so it's easy for you to coordinate outfits. Get rid of things that don't fit your new image. And I'd like your permission to go shopping for you. Better yet, we'll go shopping together." Her smile was magnificent and sent my heart racing.

A day of shopping would be hell...with anyone but her.

"Did you just manipulate me into letting you style me again? Permanently?" I said.

"I did, sweetie. Expertly, I might add."

I grimaced. "Are you going to get rid of all my comfy clothes?"

"Absolutely not. Only the ratty ones."

"Shit," I said beneath my breath, but I was unaccountably happy.

"So? What do you say?" She bit her lip in that adorable way.

"You have a deal. As long as you get rid of that awful gray blouse."

"You're on." She grabbed the hem of her blouse, pulled it off over her head, and tossed it away. "Satisfied?"

I swallowed hard as it fluttered to the floor, trying not to stare at her breasts that were pushed up in a lacy bra. I felt inadequate standing there in awe of her confidence. I'd spent my entire youth hiding my scrawny body. Hell, I still didn't like wearing tank tops. Was I supposed to make a move? Kay was such a flirt that it was hard to tell.

I stuffed my hand in my pocket and covered the jewelry box that was nestled there. "You can put that back on and throw it away later." Otherwise I was going to have an erection through dinner.

She picked up her blouse with a laugh and pulled it back on, messing her hair up in the process. Even with static playing with her tousled hair, she made my blood run hot.

"Better?" she said.

"Not really. You hair's standing on end."

She smoothed it with one hand, laughed, took my hand, and pulled me toward the dining table. "In other news, I was a very good girl today. I got along famously with Magda."

"Yeah. I could tell. What else did she ask you to change in me?"

"She wanted me to change something. But it wasn't you." Kay was being cryptic. "I did *exactly* what she advised me to do. Something to surprise you! She rewarded me, us, by cooking a special dinner, your favorite, and setting a special table." She waved her hand around the dinner table like a game show model revealing a prize.

"A surprise?"

She took my arm. "Yes, and I hope you like it." She leaned her head on my shoulder. She was taking our game to a whole new level.

A silver envelope with my name on it sat at my place at the table. I pointed to it. "Is that it?"

She squeezed my arm. "It is! I hope you like it. Do you know how hard it is to surprise a billionaire?"

"No idea," I said with a wink. "I only know a few."

"Shut up, showoff." She laughed. "Open it!"

I picked it up, curious. It wasn't sealed. I pulled a card out, a romantic card covered in hearts. *Our love is unstoppable...*

My heart pounded into overdrive. This was a joke to her, an inside joke we shared. She was playing the game, creating evidence of our "undying love." Of the real quality of our marriage. But the joke was on me. I wished this shit was real.

I turned to the inside of the card slowly. *Undeniable. Unbelievable.*

A piece of paper fluttered out. I swallowed hard, trying to cover my emotions. No girl had ever given me a romantic card before. I pointed to the word *unbelievable*, which was clearly her way of joking. "I hope not."

She laughed and handed me the piece of paper that had fallen out. "Here. This is the real gift."

I stared at it. It was product page printout from Flashionista of a custom metal wall sign that said The Millers in fancy script. "What am I not getting? You ordered something from our site? Who are the Millers?"

"Not the Millers, the Greens, silly!" She shook her head. "I ordered a sign that says The Greens." Her purse sat on the console table by the door. She grabbed it, pulled out her wallet, and flashed her driver's license at me. "Does this help?"

She had a new temporary license. For a second my heart stopped. Had I missed her birthday already?

"Look closely." She pointed to her name.

Kayla Green.

I felt myself smiling. I couldn't keep it down. "You changed your name? I thought we agreed you wouldn't."

"Are you angry?" When she bit her lip like that, she was so damned kissable I almost had to look away before I did something stupid. "I'd hoped you'd be happy. Magda convinced me that if I were really in love with you, I'd want your name. It helps with the ruse, right?"

I picked her up and swung her around while she laughed. "Yes!"

We were both laughing by the time I set Kay down. I was breathless with desire.

"Glad you're happy! I decided Magda was right, even though she didn't know what she was really saying. The more I thought about it, the more I realized I needed to do it. As insurance in case that identity thief comes out of the woodwork."

There was my chance to tell her the identity-thief bitch had made contact. I couldn't make myself ruin the moment. I would take care of it.

"I'm no lawyer," Kay said. "But I thought that if my name is legally changed to yours, it makes our claim that *I'm* the one who married you that much stronger. There's a precedent that the state has already recognized ours as the legal union."

I was still holding her. "You're not only beautiful, you're brilliant. Best gift ever."

"You're easy to please. Wait until you see what Magda made us for dinner!" She pulled away from me.

I caught her hand. "I have a surprise for you, too." I pulled the velvet ring box from my pocket and popped it open before her as if I were proposing.

Her eyes went wide. "You got it early?"

I nodded.

She slid my Order of the Engineer ring off and handed it back to me, then held her hand out to me like a princess expecting me to kiss it. "Do the honors, Mr. Green."

I slid my Order of the Engineer ring back on my pinkie finger and set the jewelry box on the counter. Her fingers were slight and soft in mine as I slid the ring onto her finger.

She pulled her hand back and held it up to admire the ring. "It's beautiful! Completely dazzling. Everyone will be *so* jealous!" She threw her arms around me and gave me a throwaway kiss. Kay was easy with her affection.

I would have given anything to keep her that happy. "Anything for you, Mrs. Green. It's beautiful on your hand."

"Yes, but you're going to take this back in a year." She made an exaggerated pouty face. "It's not part of my settlement."

I wanted her to have that ring to remember me by for the rest of her life. Even more, I wanted her to stay. A million beautiful girls wouldn't make up for her. I shrugged. "Am I? Taking back the wedding ring isn't standard divorce procedure. The ring's yours, now and always." Along with my heart.

She gave me a seriously heart-melting smile and held her hand up to admire her ring again. "I'm already one of those girls, the ones who can't stop looking at their rings!" She paused. "Where's yours? Was it ready, too? Show me your hand."

I flashed my bare hand. "It was. I picked it up, but I haven't put it on yet. That's your job." I pulled small plastic bag with the ring from my pocket.

"Just a baggie? No fancy jewelry box?" She snatched it from me and dumped it into the palm of her hand. She held it close to inspect it, studying the inside of the band. She smiled as if she was up to no good. "I called up after we left the store and had it inscribed. Have you read it?"

"And ruin the surprise?" To be honest, I hadn't given my ring more than a cursory look before I jammed it in my pocket.

She held it up for me to read the tiny writing. "Go ahead. Read it out loud."

"Love, Your Trophy Wife 24/7/365, and it has our wedding date." I grinned at her joke. Yes, I got it. We had a year. "Romantic."

"And cryptic. No one but us will get the inside joke. I couldn't very well say decoy wife. Trophy wife was the best I could do. I hope you're not offended. Everyone already thinks I'm out for your money. This is my way of saying, *In your face, suckers.*" She laughed.

"Nice."

"Give me your hand." She slid my ring on. "With this ring, I promise to play the role of your loving wife for an entire year."

My new ring felt heavy on my hand, weighed down by the end date I was trying to avoid. "I may have had something inscribed in your ring, too."

Her eyes lit up. "Did you?" She pulled hers off and looked for the inscription with an eager expression. "Not for Pawning," she read aloud. She looked up at me with an incredulous, stunned expression.

Before I could react, she gave me a sudden, playful, *hard* push to the shoulder that caught me off guard and sent me staggering back a step.

"You're awful!" But she was smiling. "Simply terrible." She slid the ring on again. "You were going to let me keep the ring all along?"

I nodded. "Gotcha! You have the ring, but you'll never profit from it, evil woman."

"I suppose I deserve that for hinting at it before." Her shoulders started to shake like she was holding a laugh in. A giggle escaped. And then suddenly we were both laughing. And laughing. Until we couldn't stop.

Finally, Kayla was holding her sides. "Stop! Stop laughing so I can stop. Ouch! I actually laughed until it hurts, you turd."

I wiped my eyes. "Got you!"

"Oh, crap!" she said, as if just remembering something. "Magda's dinner will be ruined if we don't get it on the table!"

As she headed to the kitchen, she paused to pick up the dark pink ring box. "This isn't the jewelry store's box." She frowned. She was puzzling something through. She stroked the box. "This is a custom box." She looked to me for confirmation with awe in her voice.

I shrugged as if it were no big deal. She didn't know, she couldn't know, that I was a huge romantic. I would have shown her every facet of that side of me if she'd shown any indication she would welcome it.

"Is this our supposed wedding color?"

I nodded. I might have screwed up with the gesture. Shown a little too much sensitivity.

She stroked the box. "Soft. This is real velvet, not some cheap crap."

I nodded again. I knew Kay would recognize the quality. "Vintage velvet. At least forty to a hundred years old. So the saleswoman assured me. Limited edition. You can't get those boxes anymore. The company who makes them ran out of that color of vintage velvet."

"Oh, Jus." She wiped her eyes.

I couldn't tell whether she was touched by my gesture, or still wiping away tears of laughter.

"But Jus...it's deep pink. You can see it?"

I nodded.

She looked away before I could read her face. "Dinner!"

She set the box down and raced to the kitchen and pulled dinner out of the oven. "Oh, and before I forget, I had lunch with Britt today. She's throwing us a party Saturday night. I accepted for both of us. I hope that's okay?" She set a platter on the table.

"After this surprise? Anything for you." And I meant it.

"Dinner with my parents on Friday. Party with my friends on Saturday. It's like our first round of midterms. After that, we relax and unwind!"

"Sounds good to me." I joined her in the kitchen and helped her set out the rest of the meal. "How's Britt? Did you fool her and her emotional genius?" I asked as we sat at the dinner table.

Kayla shrugged. "She's not entirely onboard yet. We ran into Lazer, though, and that distracted her."

By the nervous way Kay acted, I wasn't so sure Britt was the only one who was distracted. Damn it. I was going to have to do something about Lazer.

CHAPTER SIX

Kayla

Even with that crazy inscription, Justin's ring was the most gorgeous thing I'd ever owned. It sparkled on my finger in a way that made me incredibly happy. It would have made me a whole lot happier, if, you know, the marriage had been real and he'd been the one.

As for Jus, we took the colorblindness test online together. The test was simple, but impressive. You were shown a large circle with lots of a little circles of various colors inside it, and a number made out of one or two shades of circles. The test asked what number, if any, you saw. As the test began, I had to bite my tongue not to laugh at Jus. A number would be clearly visible to me, but he either didn't see it at all, or had to

squint to make it out. And then he was unsure of his
guess.

It was funny. Weird, and cruel, that human nature
makes us laugh at other people's inabilities. As the test
progressed, it learned from Justin's answers and quick-
ly homed in on his particular color weakness. And then
a strange thing began to happen. Jus could see num-
bers in the circles that I couldn't. Which was a revela-
tion to me—in certain color situations, his vision was
more adept than mine. I began to wonder if I was the
colorblind one.

In the end, the test determined he was a moderate
deuteranope, which meant he had a red-green deficien-
cy. As a side note, my vision was normal. But Jus was
more likely to confuse mid-reds with mid-greens, light
blues with lilac, bright greens with yellows, and, most
noticeably so far, pale pinks with light gray. And obviously, certain shades of tan/brown with greens. Which
explained why he believed peanut butter was green.

The result came as no surprise. I made a note to
pick out clothes for him that would favor his coloring
and be pleasing to him. I also noted, with a heavy heap
of regret, that the pinks I so loved and looked good in
were probably going to have to be banished from my
wardrobe for the next year.

On Friday evening, I dressed for a casual dinner at
my parents' house. Mom had been driving me crazy
with texts. First complaining in a braggy way about the
commotion the news crews were causing in the neigh-
borhood. How they'd accosted Dad and her when they
left for work on Wednesday morning. And how they

were being bombarded with requests for interviews. And what could they really say about their new son-in-law when they hadn't seen him in years? And had never been more than casually introduced to him then?

And, finally, asking what Justin's favorite foods were and whether he had any food allergies. And you know what? I'd been peeved that I had to text him and ask. There were so many things a woman gaga in love with him should have known that I had no clue about. And he didn't text right back. And I'd resorted to asking Magda.

When Jus had said he was a workaholic, he hadn't been kidding. On Thursday night, he came home after I'd gone to bed. On Friday morning, he was once again gone before I woke up. Even though I set my alarm for six so I could see him off. If I hadn't woken briefly in the middle of the night and seen him next to me, I might have assumed he hadn't come home at all.

If I were the insecure type, I would have wondered whether he was avoiding me. As it was, I had to fight bouts of insecure jealousy when I thought about Ophelia working late with him, too, trying to win him away. As I said before, I don't share well, especially not my men.

He arrived home from work with just minutes to change into the jeans and shirt I'd picked out for him, and for me to give him a quick beard trim. When I was done with him, I thought he commanded attention. Any girl checking out guys would spend some time giving him the eye, even without knowing he was filthy rich.

It was June, but a series of showers had been sweeping through along with a cold front. Any native Seattleite will tell you that June can be as cold as March, sometimes colder. I dressed in jeans and a summery, floaty top from Flashionista in a light mauve that Jus said he saw and liked. I'd bought it before our "marriage." I grabbed a sweater on the way out.

Jus owned half a dozen cars. He was in the mood to drive.

"Which car will impress your parents the most?" he asked as we stood before them.

"I know nothing about cars," I said. Which was absolutely true. "You pick."

He beeped open a sporty black two-seater and held the door open for me.

Once we were on our way, I briefed Jus. "You've met my parents a couple of times, so this should be no big deal. You know what to expect."

He raised an eyebrow. "I met them briefly twice. Once when they visited you at school and once when they stopped by to see Dex's parents and I was visiting. Both times weren't much more than introductions."

"You impressed them on the phone," I said. "As we agreed before, just don't overdo it tonight. I don't want them to get too attached to you." I paused. "We'll need to stop on the way and get some flowers and wine or something. I thought of it earlier and forgot, and then thought it's just as easy to pick something up on the way. You and I want to impress them a little with our thoughtfulness."

He grinned. "Already taken care of."

I stared at him. "What?"

"I had flowers and champagne delivered to them earlier today. With a note saying how much I was looking forward to the evening."

Crap. I stared at him, stunned. I imagined him asking Ophelia to take care of it. Or maybe she reminded him in the first place. Wasn't that what efficient PAs did? I didn't want my parents having flowers she'd ordered them. I gave him the death glare. Partly because of Ophelia's probable involvement and partly because he was being too damned thoughtful with or without it. "Anything else I should know?"

He grinned. "This car is guaranteed to impress them with its subtle elegance."

"Shut up!" I laughed. The car was anything but subtle, in my opinion.

"Okay, a few facts you should know. My parents are casual people and usually confident. Mom's a corporate lawyer and Dad's a general practitioner. They're comfortably upper middle class. But they've never met a billionaire before. They're going to be out of their element, especially since you're their son-in-law now. It's going to be an awkward dynamic, as you heard on the phone when I told them about you. Usually the parents are in the more secure financial position."

He nodded, and, frankly, looked a little nervous. I was trying to put him at ease. He had the power position here.

"The goal tonight is to get *mildly* acquainted with them. Get on their good side, but don't overdo it. You don't want them to get too fond of you. You're only their son-in-law for a year. After that, sorry, but you're going to be the scapegoat. I'm going to have to pin the demise on our marriage on someone, and they'll take my side no matter what, so it may as well be you."

"Gee, thanks."

I laughed. "Oh, shut up! Your parents will do the same and blame me. Only you'll be a hero in their eyes once they find out I only walk away with a paltry ten mil."

He opened his mouth like he was about to say something.

I cut him off. "A few things to keep in mind. Avoid the usual taboo topics like politics. Dad *loves* to talk politics and will bait you and try to draw you into a political debate so he can eviscerate you. He was a champion debater. Don't fall for his traps."

I took a quick breath. "Mom and Dad love games, board games especially. But they are cutthroat and show *no* mercy. Absolutely none. At some point, they'll want us to play something. If that happens, follow my lead. We'll try to escape without playing. If we somehow get trapped into it, I'll angle for the most cooperative game I can. Though they really only own one, Pandemic. Which I gave them. Dad, being a doctor, can sometimes be talked into playing it—"

Jus grabbed my hand. "Slow down. It's okay, Kay. Everything will be fine. I can handle myself."

I was more nervous than I thought. I squeezed his hand. "We should have brought Data with us. She'd distract Mom and Dad."

Half an hour later, we were walking up to my parents' front door. Mercifully, there were no news crews in sight. The door swung open before I could let us in.

"Kayla!" Mom pulled me into a hug while Dad waited his turn and Jus stood off to the side.

I hugged Dad and looped my arm through Justin's. "Mom and Dad, you remember Justin."

He offered his hand to Dad while Mom studied him.

"This is awkward," Jus said to Dad in that startlingly deep, smooth voice of his. "Now that I'm married to your daughter, what would you like me to call you, Mr. Lucas? We should get that settled straight off. So I don't have to do contortions trying not to use your name or call you Hey You."

Dad laughed, obviously charmed. Mom tittered nervously as Jus hugged her warmly. And I wondered where the hell Jus had gone to charm school.

"What is Kayla calling your parents?" Mom asked.

I shrugged. "I haven't met Justin's dad. I call his mom Diana."

"You've met his mom?" Her voice was heavy on the accusation: *Before we got to see Justin?*

Oops! I'd slipped up and put Mom in a huff. "She dropped by unexpectedly." Wasn't I supposed to be the suave one here?

My response put Mom at ease, but only a little. Although there was a gleam of admiration for Diana in her eye that indicated she wished she'd thought of that. While at the same time, she smirked as if to say she and Dad were classier than to surprise attack their new son-in-law.

"Call me Debbie, if you like, Justin," Mom said. "But I really *hope* you'll call me Mom."

Damn. Damn, damn, damn. There was that competitive edge showing, and I'd walked right into it.

Jus beamed at her. "It would be my pleasure...Mom."

She beamed back. I wanted to smack them both. This would not end well.

"I was going to suggest Don or Doc. Guess that makes me Dad now," Dad said. But he was smiling broadly.

Mom had been taking Justin's measure. "It's been at least several years since we've seen you. You've...matured a lot since we last saw you, Justin."

His answering laugh was deep and sweet. "You mean I've grown. About six inches. And a beard. It startles everyone."

Mom and Dad laughed with him. But I could tell Mom was not a fan of the bushy beard. Close-cropped, styled beards could be sexy, in Mom's opinion, and mine. Yes, I'd trimmed Justin's beard, but it was still just a well-trimmed bush that covered his face. I was still holding out a faint hope that once the heat of summer set in, he'd shave it for comfort.

"Kayla, let's see that famous ring that's been on the news!" Mom held her hand out for mine.

I wiggled my ring finger and extended my hand like a queen for Mom to admire.

As Mom took my hand in hers, she gasped softly. "The pictures in the news didn't do it justice. It's much more gorgeous in person." She gave me a quick hug.

I was both touched and worried that Mom had been following the news about us so closely. I felt the tight wire we were walking beneath my feet as keenly as if it were real. My chest squeezed tight. The stress was killing me.

A week ago, I'd just been another dumped girl. Now every move I made was subject to scrutiny, even with my parents'. My life really was a stage, a constant act. And I had continuous stage fright. At any minute I worried I'd slip up and forget my lines.

"Come on in." Mom touched Justin's arm. "Thank you for the gorgeous flowers you sent this afternoon. Roses and daylilies are my favorite!" She turned to me. "Kayla, you'll have to come see them. Your husband is the most thoughtful young man."

Why was she so certain I had nothing to do with them? We followed her to the dining room, where the flowers took center stage on the table. It was, indeed, an awesome bouquet in a vase that matched the colors and décor of the house.

A chill crawled down my back. If this selection was pure dumb luck, I'd eat my purse. He had to have researched what Mom liked and what the house looked like. Had I posted any pictures on social media? I didn't think so. Had Mom? I honestly couldn't remember. His computer skills were a little too awesome and powerful.

Mom leaned in and whispered for my ears only, "I know you must have guided him in his choices, but it's still sweet of him to be thoughtful enough to ask what we like and what our style is."

Hers was a natural assumption. Why *hadn't* he asked me?

She stepped back and spoke in a normal volume. "Look at the card Justin sent with it." Mom handed me one of those Flashionista thank-you cards that came with your order. Handwritten in Justin's block printing was a note. *Thanks for raising such a beautiful woman to be my bride. Looking forward to dinner. Love, Justin*

I wanted to gag. And kill Jus. So that's why she knew I, at the very least, hadn't sent the note. It sounded nothing like me. It was so thoughtful that it was sickening. And the writing was clearly Justin's.

And that's the way it went through dinner. Jus turned on charm I didn't know he possessed while my parents grilled him mercilessly. He answered all their questions with as much aplomb and acumen as I imagined he'd handled his rounds with angel investors. He looked at me adoringly. Held my hand. Looped his arm around me. He made them fall in love with him through the sheer magnetism of his will and personality. Damn if I knew how he did it. Somewhere along the way to becoming a billionaire, he'd developed charisma.

I kept trying to signal him to tone it down. He ignored me. He was suddenly the son they'd never had and always wanted. He laughed at Mom's horrible corporate contract law jokes and tales of her nerdy coworkers. Smiled and sympathized at Dad's stories about all the things he'd pulled out of kids' nostrils and ears over the years. He complimented Mom's cooking, the house, and her outfit. Somehow without laying it on too thick.

He looked at me adoringly, beaming like a guy in love who simply couldn't force the smile down. Like a groom at his wedding.

Halfway through dinner, Mom turned to Jus. "Justin, I'm dying to know—how did you propose?"

Jus paused with a fork halfway to his mouth.

I set my glass down harder than I'd intended. "Yeah, tell them the story, sweetie. It's so cute." Me sick with food poisoning while he married an imposter. It was the stuff of romantic fairy tales.

Jus grabbed my hand and squeezed it. "You tell it better than I do."

I raised an eyebrow, ready to kill him. "People prefer to hear it from the groom's mouth. What possesses a guy to propose just hours after seeing a girl for the first time in years?" I really wanted to know. More accurately, I wanted to know what possessed him to marry the imposter.

He froze. I was enjoying his discomfort. Let him be firmly in the hot seat in my life for once. Let him make up stories without tripping up. And have his life totally interrupted. And really have to act instead of disappearing into life as normal.

He smiled at me, so deeply it reached his eyes, before he focused his attention on Mom. "Have you ever had a friend that you don't see often, but whenever you do, you connect? It's as if you haven't been apart. You feel as close as ever."

Mom leaned forward, listening with rapt attention. She and Dad both nodded.

"That's what it's like between Kay and me. Only deeper. More passionate. When I spotted her in the hotel, I had to ask her to go out for a drink. When I found out she was single, I knew I had to seize my opportunity to catch her between guys or lose her. I knew it was right. I didn't have time to think it out or plan something romantic. As we were leaving the restaurant, I couldn't let her go. I just blurted out, 'We feel right together. Let's get married. Tonight. In this perfect moment.' And she agreed."

Crap, he was good. My parents turned to me for confirmation. Mom had tears in her eyes. Dad still looked skeptical.

"Kayla?" Mom asked.

"What can I add? It was simple and sweet." I smiled as if I couldn't be happier, and leaned my head on his shoulder.

Mom studied me. "It's not how you used to describe your perfect marriage proposal."

"When you find the right one, any proposal he makes is perfect." I wasn't sure I believed that. But Mom seemed to buy it.

After dinner, Jus helped clear the dishes, just like family.

Mom whispered to me, "He's certainly blossomed. He's obviously in love with you. I always admit when I'm wrong. Well, I was wrong. Seeing him with my own eyes, I understand how he could sweep you off your feet in an evening. Just his voice!" She looked upward and sighed in that way women do when they're in love with something.

My parents weren't superficial, shallow people. They weren't suckers for praise or shameless flattery. They usually saw right through it. And disdained and mocked it later in private. Jus was just good. Genuinely considerate and kind. Personable. For their part, Mom and Dad were trying hard and giving him every benefit of the doubt. For my sake, I realized. They wanted to love him because I'd "chosen" him, at least as far as they knew.

They were also generally concerned, considerate parents who had a history of accurately assessing friends and boyfriends. They tried to warn me off Eric the very first time they met him, way before he became a total douchebag. In eighth grade, they warned me my new bestie was out for herself and would turn out to be a backstabber. Time, and not much of it, proved them right.

That they were falling for Jus sent me into a guilty panic. I tried to tamp it down.

"I got something special for dessert," Mom said. "You two have a seat while I bring it out. Don, get the champagne Justin sent with the flowers. Would anyone like coffee, too?"

"I'll get the coffee, Mom." I started to get out of my seat.

"No, just sit! I'll get everything." She seemed excited about something. Mom disappeared into the kitchen and reappeared carrying a nine-inch layered wedding cake topped with a ceramic bride and groom. The groom held the bride in his arms while the bride stared lovingly into his eyes and touched his face. She set the cake on the table before us. "Happy one-week anniversary!"

Crap. It was our purported one-week anniversary.

"Mom, that's beautiful. You shouldn't have," I said, trying to beat Jus to the punch.

"I wanted to see my baby girl cut her cake. Hang on!" She disappeared and returned carrying a silver tray, her best china dessert plates, pink napkins, and a silver knife and cake server with perfect ribbon bows tied around them. "Those are the serving set from *our* wedding." She was beaming.

Jus had passed some kind of test, obviously. If he hadn't, I doubted we'd have gotten the cake and the use of her sentimental cake knife and server.

Dad walked in from the kitchen behind her, carrying a bottle of expensive champagne and four champagne flutes, two tied with bows around their stems and engraved. He set the engraved flutes in front of us. They had our names and our wedding date on them. I got a lump in my throat. I hadn't expected this.

"Wait! Let me get my camera." Mom hurried off to get it, returning a second later as if she'd had it ready and waiting nearby. "Okay, you two newlyweds. Cut the cake!"

"I think we need to stand for this." Jus pulled me to my feet and wrapped his arms around me, grabbing the cake knife so that we both held it. He poised it over the cake.

"Hold that pose!" Mom said. "Let me get a few stills of you. Then I'm going to record."

My heart hammered in my ears as I smiled for the camera, trying desperately to look like a woman who was desperately in love. My mouth was dry. If I hadn't felt so guilty, I might even have enjoyed myself.

"Got it! Cut the cake." Mom kept the camera on us.

"Ready?" Jus whispered in my ear.

He smelled good. His arms were strong and steady around me. I pushed my fears aside and let his solid, square hands guide mine as we sliced into the cake. And awkwardly flopped a piece on one of Mom's dessert plates. And got frosting all over our fingers as the slice nearly slid off onto the floor and we caught it together.

As I reached for a napkin to wipe my fingers, Jus grabbed my hand and pulled into to his mouth, sucking the frosting off my fingers before I could pull away. Caressing them with his hot tongue.

"Very romantic and sweet," Mom said, still filming. "But frosting doesn't count as the first bite. Lala, feed Justin a piece of cake."

Crap. I was still tingling from the way he'd sucked my fingers and thrust his tongue between them, knowing I wouldn't squirm in front of my parents.

I played along. Determined to get him back, I broke off a small piece and held it between my fingers. "Open wide, babe."

I grinned evilly. Let him feel the fear. What would I do? How would I play this cake feeding to make it different from the one at Lazer Lodge? Feeding each other cake defined the tone of your marriage. Were you light and playful? Serious and classy? Out to get each other? Did you stuff it in each other's face? Delicately, lovingly feed each other? Joke around? Use a fork? Or the intimacy of your fingers?

I was already using my fingers. His gaze held mine as he, too, took a bite of cake in hand. Yes, we were at each other's mercy.

I should have looked away. But I was mesmerized. His hand reached toward my mouth. Mine toward his. As if we were playing a game of wedding cake chicken. I knew instinctively he would mimic what I did. At the last second, I went for classy and loving, and set the cake gently on his tongue. And he did the same.

My bite was a little too large for my mouth. As I put my hand beneath my chin to catch any falling crumbs, Jus wiped a blob of frosting from his finger onto my nose.

Dad laughed. Mom clapped.

I would have protested. If I hadn't had a mouthful of cake. Which I was sure was the intent. Jus grabbed me and dipped me over his arm, giving me a dramatic kiss. When he pulled me back up, he wiped the frosting off my nose.

"You have crumbs in your beard." I shouldn't have laughed. But he was manipulating me in such a funny, charming way.

Dad poured champagne. When everyone had a glass, he lifted his to us. "To Kayla and Justin. May they always be as much in love as they are today!"

Oh, Daddy. You don't know how much you just cursed us.

Mom gently pushed us out of the way and began cutting cake. "This is just a dry run for your reception. We desperately need to plan one, Lala."

I paled and broke out in a cold sweat as I pictured my grandparents, aunts, uncles, and cousins toasting us. Bringing us gifts I'd have to return in a year. I mean, if a marriage only lasts a year, wasn't it polite to return the presents? I would have to look it up. I pictured Jus charming them, worming his way into their good graces only to betray them later.

I felt the noose tightening. My independence slipping away. Mom was still chattering on about plans. "No!" I shook my head, vehement. "No! No reception."

"Kayla Marie! What's wrong with you?" Mom stared at me as if I were an alien being.

I'd never liked betraying people. "No. People will feel obligated to bring presents. And we don't need anything. Even if we tell them not to, they will. No. I just don't...no." I began shaking so badly I had to set my champagne down.

Jus was the only one who understood. I threw myself into his arms, fighting back a sob. He cradled me tenderly, running his fingers through my hair and gently murmuring reassurances.

I'd never had an anxiety attack before, but this sure felt like one. "This is why we eloped!" I said into his shirt. "To avoid all the hassles of a wedding. Being a billionaire, Jus is in a unique situation. People expect more, more of everything for a billionaire's wedding.

The press wants a piece. And ordinary people, like our friends and family, feel out of their element. No. I won't put people through it."

I tore away enough to look at Mom and Dad. "We don't want to put you through the expense and hassle. Please." I gulped. My voice sounded tiny. "No reception."

Mom's stunned expression turned to admiration. It was like a light bulb had gone off for her. Ah-hah! Now she understood why I'd eloped. I had a logical reason, good rationale. That made me look mature and selfless. And as if I wasn't mercenary at all. My panic and guilt had just made me look like a good, considerate person.

Jus nodded. "Kay and I are united in this."

Mom nodded. "Okay then. No more talk of it. For now. The rest of the family will want to meet you someday, Justin." She was smiling as if she was proud of me. "When are you two taking your honeymoon?"

A vacations sounds good, I thought. Jus and I needed some time to get to know each other.

"We haven't made any plans yet." Jus sounded so casual. "As soon as I can break away, which may not be until fall. But will have to be before the holiday season. Once that hits, I'll wish I didn't need to sleep."

"Where are you thinking of?" Mom said. "Europe in the fall is beautiful—"

Dad cut in. "They'll figure it out, Debbie. Who's up for a rousing board game?" He named the game that had nearly ended my parents' marriage less than a month after the wedding.

"Sounds great!" Jus said before I could stop him.

He couldn't know the history. Unless his cyber snooping had told him that, too.

"Nice try, Dad," I said. "I think Jus has passed enough of your tests tonight. I'm not playing that game with Jus. Not ever. Are you trying to drive us to divorce court?"

Dad laughed.

Jus gave me a puzzled look.

"You almost walked into a trap." I gave him the condensed version of what had happened.

He grabbed my hand and squeezed it. "Bring it on. We're up for it."

"No. We're not. Jus, we don't have to prove ourselves."

An evil thought crossed my mind. Wouldn't it be fun to play that particular fight-inducing game the day before our divorce and then blame our breakup on it? Wouldn't Mom and Dad feel guilty then?

Eh. They'd probably just say we should have played tonight, at the beginning, before wasting time on a doomed relationship. That how you treated each other while you played told a lot about a relationship.

CHAPTER SEVEN

Justin

"What were you doing in there?" Kayla threw her hands up as we pulled out of her parents' driveway.

"What do you mean?" I cringed, genuinely puzzled. Why was she upset with *me*? The evening had been a success as far as I could tell. I'd done all the socially expected things.

"Going all charming on my parents. Sending them *flowers*." Emphasis as if flowers was a dirty word. She crossed her arms and rolled her eyes like I'd committed a capital crime against floral arrangements. Sent them into a war zone or something equally heinous. "You weren't supposed to be *that* nice to them!"

"I wasn't being *that* nice. Just considerate. People bring flowers when they go to someone's house for dinner."

"Yeah. Bring. Not send horribly expensive arrangements thoughtfully picked to complement the hostess' décor."

I still didn't understand her wrath. "I thought that's what you wanted?"

She sighed as if she was totally exasperated with me. As if I were a complete douche. "Polite and distant. You were supposed to be *polite* and *distant*. That's it. *Nothing* more. Nothing extraordinary."

"I wasn't being extraordinary. I picked a very reasonably priced arrangement. I made an effort not to go wild and send them something so expensive they'd be embarrassed to accept it. And I only had it delivered because I didn't have time to go shopping myself. Ordering from a website is a hell of a lot less thoughtful than picking something out in person. It's so easy, it's practically selfish. Have credit card, will shop online."

She made a growling sound in the back of her throat and gave me a death glare an evil emperor would have been proud of.

Sometimes arguments, over totally silly shit, just spiral out of control. We were still going round and round about my behavior, neither of us seeing the other's point of view, as we walked into the penthouse.

Kayla ignored Data when she came running, barking happily to greet us.

I scooped Data up. "Come on, Kay. You're not being fair. Any other couple would consider the evening a success. *I* think it *was* a success. We fooled your parents. We won them over. They're on our side. They believe this marriage is real. That's what we want."

"That's what *you* want." Her voice was hard as she took off her sweater and tossed it over the back of the sofa.

"Be reasonable—"

She spun and faced me. "This is on *your* head. I asked you to be polite. Be pleasant. But keep your distance. *You* had to go over the top. You had to be as competitive as they are. You just had to ingratiate yourself with them. Had to impress them. Don't you see?"

Her eyes were fierce. Her face was set. "I love them. For all their faults, they're *my* parents. I don't want to see them get hurt. Not them. Nor my grandparents. Nor my cousins. But especially not Mom and Dad. They're the ones who are going to ache for me when this"—she pointed between her and me—"this *thing* is over.

"You're not supposed to be the lovable billionaire son-in-law that broke my heart. Who got away. I'm not supposed to be the villain here. When all is said and done, *you are.*"

The venom in her voice stung.

I took a deep breath. I'd screwed up again. "Kay, I'm sorry. I thought I was just being polite."

She put her hands on her hips and glared at me so hard that Data dug in and whimpered in my arms.

I scratched her chin. "She's not scolding you, girl."

Kayla's face softened. She threw up her hands. "Sending Mom her favorite flowers? That's not playing up to them? How in the world did you know, anyway? Are you cyber-stalking my life and family?"

"Cyber-stalk? Come on, Kay. Give me some credit." I swallowed hard. "I have an incredibly good memory and I pay attention." Unlike some people. "I remember everything you've told me about them."

I had no other defense. My ears picked up when her cousin Dex talked about Kayla's family, their house, their vacation. I remembered the pictures she'd shown me in college.

I was a creepy freak. A rich douche. A guy who had no clue about girls.

Her face softened. "I told you what Mom's favorite flowers are?"

I nodded. "In college. You were trying to decide if you should get her some for Mom's Weekend."

Her eyes went wide. "And their house?" She faltered. "How did you know how it was decorated?"

"You showed me pictures when they were remodeling."

"Crap!" She frowned like she was trying to remember. Suddenly her face cleared. "I did, didn't I? I'd forgotten."

I shrugged, trying to be the bigger man.

She took a deep breath and put the back of her hand to her head. "I'm sorry, Jus. This is all so confusing. I'm overreacting. Thinking about a reception and fooling everyone I love just sent me over the edge."

"It's okay," I said. "We're just feeling our way through this. We'll get better at it."

She gave me a small smile and blinked back tears, probably of frustration. With me.

She nodded. "You're right. Thanks for backing me up about the reception. I didn't really even ask what you think. Do you want a reception?"

I shook my head. "Not if you don't."

She nodded again. "Good. Thanks." She paused. "It's been a long day. I'm going to bed. Are you coming?"

I shook my head. "I have work to do."

She frowned. I'd stepped in it again.

"Working on Friday night?" She snorted softly and shook her head like she didn't understand me at all.

The feeling was mutual.

She stared at me like I was an alien being from the planet Weirdo. "Are you twenty-one or forty?"

Her question took me aback. "Billion-dollar retail empires don't run themselves."

She shook her head. "You should be drinking. And partying. And chasing girls. Jus, you shouldn't even be out of college yet."

I swallowed hard. *Shit.* In her eyes, I was a baby. "Is that what you *want* me to be doing? Acting like I'm some immature frat guy?" Her accusation hit me hard. I spat the words out without thinking. "You want me to be like Eric?"

Her face fell.

I wanted to take the words back the moment I spoke them.

She shook her head. "I have no right to judge. I don't understand your world. I have no idea what it takes to do what you do. The thought of all that responsibility is too much." She hesitated. "When *is* your birthday?"

No, she really wouldn't understand how I knew so much about her. She'd obviously paid no attention to me. Maybe I *was* obsessed with her. "August twenty-second. It's my golden birthday this year. Twenty-two on the twenty-second. Or my champagne birthday, as Mom says. She's big into finding special significance in every birthday she can. She likes birthdays."

Kay actually smiled a little, but it looked sad. "You're such a nerd, Jus." She took a step toward me, took my face in her hands, and gave me a kiss. "Always kiss goodnight. Even when you're upset with each other," she whispered.

I loved her. More than ever. I'd meant what I'd said about our supposed proposal. With Kayla, things felt right. I wished she would see it that way. I wanted her to kiss me goodnight every night. Not just as part of a routine. Or to keep up pretenses. But because she wanted to. Because she loved me.

"Goodnight, Jus."

Data barked. Kayla reached over and scratched her head. When Data barked again, still not satisfied with the level of affection she was getting, Kay bent and let Data give her a licky dog kiss, laughing infectiously. She stood up straight and grinned at me. "Aren't you glad I kissed you first?"

"I don't know," I said. "I like dog kisses."

She laughed again and walked away with that sexy-as-hell sway of hers.

I put Data in her bed, went into my office, and closed the door. I sat at my desk, thinking. I'd been avoiding going to bed at the same time as Kayla. I'd been intentionally sleeping next to her as little as possible, going to bed after she was asleep. Getting up before she did. Part of the reason was my impossible schedule and my quest to find the ID thief. The rest was my insecurity.

I spent my nights wide awake, wanting to touch her. I slept with a hard-on. I woke with a hard-on. I balled my fists so hard they hurt, and my short nails dug into my palms, all to keep from touching her. I went to bed late and got up early to hide my horniness from her.

Commercials for male vitality say you should see your doctor if you have an erection lasting more than four hours. Mine lasted twenty-four-seven when I was around Kay. That was how it felt, anyway. Maybe I needed treatment. What the hell did they do for a perpetual boner, anyway? For a guy who was hopelessly in love with a girl who couldn't see how good he would be to her and was way out of his league?

I was as sexually frustrated and horny as any guy on the planet. Hell, maybe the universe.

I was trying to respect the terms of our agreement. Show her I respected her. And, if I was being honest, I couldn't face being vulnerable with her again. Not until I had a hint that she reciprocated my feelings, even the slightest bit. That she felt *some* sexual attraction to me.

I was still stung from the time in college when I'd made a move on her. An awkward move. She put me in my place. Gently. But definitely firmly. It was embarrassing as hell.

I had another insecurity. I was still a virgin. A virgin who'd studied the subject in all the detail guys will. Who'd read enough how-to, I hoped to have some clue what I was doing. But instruction manuals only go so far. And she'd slept with the *masterful* Eric for years. The stud, as she'd described him more times than I liked to remember.

Call me an accidental virgin. It's not as if I hadn't wanted to get laid. It's more like I'd failed in the attempts. I never really dated. Who wanted to date a boyish nerd? And sleep with one? Shit, not the kind of girl I wanted. Once I started Flash, I was too busy to worry about women. Now I was paying the price of inexperience.

I could go to a prostitute. Get a high-class call girl. Wouldn't that be a great story for the gossip-hungry press? Seattle's biggest nerd can't get laid. Arrested for solicitation a week after wedding on a whim.

Kay would kill me. And divorce me. Leaving me and Flash to the mercy of that ID bitch.

So I lived with my twenty-four-hour boner and my hope that Kayla would fall in love with me, wishing I could tell her how I felt about her. That the last week had only rekindled what I'd felt for her in college. That she made me smile. Made my heart race. Made my day. That we were perfectly suited to each other. If only she would see it. I waited for the day closer to our first anniversary when I could make my move. And withstand the rejection if she walked out on me.

I opened my desk drawer and pulled out a romantic greeting card I'd bought to give Kayla with her wedding ring. At the last minute, I'd decided it was too much. But now I had things to tell her. Things she had to know before she divorced me. I grabbed a pen and began to write.

As I poured out my thoughts, the facial recognition running on my computer came up with a match to my face and the bar I'd been at with the Kayla imposter. My heart skidded to a stop. My mouth went dry as I stared into the face of the woman I'd actually married.

Shit. I took a long, deep breath to calm my excitement.

Once I neutralized the threat of this woman, I would go after Kay.

Kayla

Jus got up early and went to the office Saturday morning. He woke me to tell me he was leaving.

I pushed my hair out of my eyes. "Don't forget. We have Britt's party tonight."

"I'm not going to spend the whole day at the office. Just a few hours. I have a couple of things to take care of. I'll be back early this afternoon. I promise."

I nodded and fell back to sleep. After I got up and showered, I went to the closet where my clothes, the few I'd managed to cram in, were stuffed into a tiny corner behind rows of jeans and crap. The rest of my things were still on the red chair or in my suitcases.

I stared at that closet, getting angrier and angrier. I was tired of being plucked out of my life and dropped into Justin's without any thought. Without any consideration for my needs. Without feeling like I belonged. I deserved a spot in it, a real place. And enough of the closet so I didn't feel like a squatter for the remainder of our marriage.

I furiously attacked Justin's closet. When I was through with it, it would be organized, I would have plenty of room, and Jus would have a decent wardrobe and system for picking out clothes without my help.

I pulled a lightweight jacket out and frowned. Whoever thought this was fashionable needed a lesson in style. I rolled my eyes. Ophie had probably picked it out.

Before I tossed it onto the donate pile, I went through the pockets. Was I hoping for cash? I laughed to myself. Maybe.

No cash, but I pulled a sealed greeting card envelope out of the breast pocket, thinking it was something Justin had forgotten to mail.

To My Wife Kayla, to be read the day before our divorce.

My pulse raced. What treasure was this? Or was it a curse? The card shook in my hand. A war raged inside me. To open? Or not?

Gina Robinson is the award-winning author of the contemporary new adult romances *Rushed, Crushed, Reckless Longing, Reckless Secrets,* and *Reckless Together* and the Agent Ex series of humorous romantic suspense novels. She's currently working on the next installment of Switched at Marriage.

Connect with Gina Online:

My Website: http://www.ginarobinson.com/
Twitter: @ginamrobinson
Facebook: www.facebook.com/GinaRobinsonAuthor